# Max Chambers P.I.

# Max Chambers P.I.

## The Case of the Nazi Ghost

## Michael J. Cinelli

| Library of Congress Control Number: | | 2017912265 |
|---|---|---|
| ISBN: | Hardcover | 978-1-5434-4263-2 |
| | Softcover | 978-1-5434-4264-9 |
| | eBook | 978-1-5434-4265-6 |

Print information available on the last page.

Rev. date: 08/03/2017

**To order additional copies of this book, contact:**
Xlibris
1-888-795-4274
www.Xlibris.com
Orders@Xlibris.com
761806

# CONTENTS

*To my wife and children.*

To my son, Michael, the angry young man. Keep fighting the good fight and waving those flags of discontent.

To my daughter, Katherine, my muse and inspiration. Your encouragement got the words out of my mind and onto the paper.

To my wife, Annamarie, the love of my life. You're the strongest and bravest woman I have ever known. You kicked cancer's ass!

# Prologue

Germany
April 11, 1945

O n any other day, the beautiful German countryside would be perfect for a picnic. Lush green fields were dotted with thick leafy shade trees. Something didn't smell right though. Literally, it didn't smell right. There must have been a bombed-out horse stable upwind of the squad. It stank. Rotting carcasses were something that were a constant in the war. From Normandy to Paris through Belgium and into Germany, scenic landscapes were dotted with craters of smoking ruin. Other landscapes were gone forever, laid waste to the destruction of the war.

Gen. George S. Patton's Eighty-Ninth Infantry Division was making its way across Europe, leaving its share of carnage in its wake. "Old Blood and Guts" wanted to get to Berlin ahead of the British general Bernard "Monty" Montgomery. The two men hated each other. Montgomery thought Patton was a glory hound. Patton thought Monty was overrated. Each man had a point. Patton had actually raced faster than his supply lines. His tanks had nearly run out of gas. He now had to depend on foot patrols.

Sgt. John Murray was leading one of these patrols through that beautiful German countryside. A seasoned veteran, Murray had seen action in North Africa, Italy, the D-day invasion of Normandy, the Hürtgen Forest in Belgium, and the Battle of the Bulge. His squad was mostly made up of green kids, and he wanted to keep them safe. He took things slow, making precise and calculated moves. Most of the rookies didn't like it. They wanted to see action, kill Nazis, and go home a hero. A few were thankful for the slow approach. They were nervous and scared and just wanted to make it home—hero or not.

Pvt. Max Chambers was one who preferred Sergeant Murray. He was drafted along with his buddy, Jimmy Kemp, and his fellow private wanted the glory. He usually volunteered to take point on patrols and was quick to fire his Thompson "Tommy Gun." Also in the squad were Pvts. Lew Frazier, Alvin Barry, Nick Rapowski, and John Santori. Cpl. Tim Golding, a D-day vet, was another steadying force.

Suddenly, the peaceful day took a deadly turn. Shots rang out, and Corporal Golding fell dead, shot through the face. Everyone hit the deck with Kemp spraying the field wildly. Sergeant Murray, spotting the source of the shots, called for grenades. Barry had the best arm and landed three in the heart of the nest. A white flag arose from the smoke, and cease-fire was called.

"Come out," Murray called. Max wasn't sure whether he said it in German. "Raus!" was what he said next. Two soldiers emerged from the smoking nest. Kemp and Frazier stripped them of any weapons and dragged them over.

They were kids. Max thought they must have been about fourteen years old. One had pissed himself. They smelled like they must have been with the horses but much worse. *Maybe the horses were dead and rotting,* Max thought. He couldn't get over that smell. Sergeant Murray got them to give the locale of their camp, just over the hill.

"Call in to HQ and get some reinforcements up here," called Sergeant Murray.

"Radio's toast," said Private Santori. "Took a hit."

"All right, tie up these two and bring up the rear."

"Yes, sir."

"Don't call me sir, Santori," Murray said with a grin.

The squad made their way down a dirt road and found the camp. Two guard towers stood tall in the noon sun, but little else was evident. Huge metal gates blocked the entrance, but there were no guards.

"Rapowski, get in the trees over there and take out the guard towers. Got your BAR?"

"Got it." Rapowski was a little guy, but he carried his Browning automatic rifle as though it was a part of him.

"Kemp, you take point. Barry, go left. Chambers, go right, and I'll take center. When Rapowski fires, we'll blow the gates with grenades. Lay down some smoke and take cover once you're in. Got it? We're waiting on you, Rapowski," said the sergeant.

It all seemed to go like clockwork. The two guards in the towers dropped almost simultaneously. The gates blew open wide. Max, Barry, and Kemp made their way in, Rapowski covering fire, and Santori blew open a blockhouse with a perfectly placed grenade. Sergeant Murray, on his belly at the gates, emptied his Thompson into the blockhouse. Shouts of "Nien nien" came from within, and a white flag was waving from a window.

"Come out, RAUS! You fuckers!" screamed Kemp. Slowly, a line of men and women streamed from the building.

Max looked for Sergeant Murray but found him still on his belly at the gates. "You hit, Sarge?"

"Uh-huh" was all he could say.

"Santori, get over here with the first aid kit!" Max screamed.

"Don't bother. You're in charge, Chambers," said the sergeant.

"In charge of what? I'm just a private!"

"Take over. Do it like I did, like I showed you, Max," Sergeant Murray said thickly. Those were his last words. Max went to check his pulse but stopped when he saw the sergeant's chest was ripped open. He held back a gag and stood, waving off Santori. Max motioned to another blockhouse.

It had been silent this whole time, but Max would take no chances now that it was his decisions on the line. With Kemp and Frazier guarding the prisoners, Max, Barry, and Santori prepared to open it up. It was just a thin door that Max kicked in with a deep breath he ran in, his comrades on either side. It was another deep breath that stopped him in his tracks. An unimaginable odor slapped his face, followed by a vision of skeletons, walking skeletons. Checking his mates, he saw that they had stopped cold too. The building was filled with sobbing men, most too weak to stand.

They were skin and bone—literally. He had never seen anything like it. It seemed impossible that they were still alive. They wore rags or nothing at all. "America, Americans," they were saying through tears and moans. That stink that the two kids reeked of was this, death, the walking death that was all around him. They were trying to lift him and his mates onto their shoulders but were too weak to do.

Max pulled away and went into the courtyard. "Breathe," he told himself, "breathe deep. Get your head back." What would the sarge do now?

"Rapowski, are we secure?"

"Yeah, Max," he said. "Sergeant Murray?"

"No," Max said, shaking his head. "Put me in charge. Start getting these people out of that building. Tell Barry and Santori."

"Check."

"Jimmy," Max called out. Kemp came running over.

"I secured all the prisoners," he said.

"Sergeant's dead. He put me in charge."

"You? I'm on point every time, and he put you in charge?"

"Don't give me any grief, man. This is all too much for us."

Just then, the bedraggled residents of the camp found the strength they lacked earlier. They returned the misery and torture that they had endured. They attacked the kneeling Germans. Shots rang out. When Max got there, he found that Frazier had given his sidearm to one of the men in rags. Two guards lay dead. "Take back that weapon!" he shouted. "Everyone stop!"

Max grabbed one of the Nazis. "What goes on here? Who is your commandant?"

"I am," said one of the Nazis as he stood.

"Who are all these people?"

"They are only Jews. We have done the world a great service. You should be thanking me now," he said with a smug smile on his face.

Max's hand tightened around the Nazi's throat. "Thank you? You want me to thank you? FUCK YOU!" With that, Max threw him to the waiting hands of the mob. They grabbed at him from every direction, beating at him, tearing at him.

"Nien, nien," he cried. "Hilf me mein Got! Hilf!" They tore him to pieces. Max watched the spectacle until the German was dead.

"Kemp, Frazier, load these Nazis into one of those trucks and get 'em out of here. You know the way back to camp," Max said. As they walked past him to the truck, one of the Nazis spat at Max's feet.

"Jew lover."

Max grabbed him by the throat and slapped him in the face—and again. He looked into the gray eyes of the Nazi and saw such evil and hatred. He slapped him again and was ready to throw him to the mob but stopped himself.

"You're gonna hang for this, and I'm gonna watch!" He pushed him to the truck.

Women guards climbed in last. Max couldn't believe a woman could be a part of this madness. As Max watched the truck drive off, his pal Jimmy Kemp gave him the dirtiest look.

The second and third squads arrived. *Great,* Max thought, *another twenty or so troops to handle the crowd and someone else to take charge, not just a lowly private. That would make Jimmy feel a little better.*

Santori ran up. "Max, it's Barry."

"What happened to him?" Max asked.

"I don't know. Come see."

Barry was on his knees, crying, sobbing uncontrollably like a grandmother, wailing. The Jews were trying to console him.

"Leave him alone," Max said. "Leave him alone."

Sergeant Millwood pulled Max aside. "You know, I heard about shit like this, but I thought it was just a lot of bunk. HQ is sending food and medics. That was a smart move getting those Krauts out of here. When did they leave?"

Max looked confused. "You should have passed them on the way in. They left about twenty minutes before you got here, Sarge."

An explosion came from over the hill. "Rapowski, see what that was."

"Check."

"Santori, see if you can find a radio here and contact HQ. We need some help over here. There must be about a thousand people."

"Okay, Max."

"We're outside of a town called Weimar. I don't know what they call this place."

"Hell?" he said.

"You know, Chambers," said Millwood, "you guys got the shit end of the stick today."

"What do you mean, Sarge?"

"This is somewhat of a sub-camp. These poor bastards took over the rest of the compound and killed most of the Nazis. Most of the Krauts deserted already."

The people swarmed around Max, crying and kissing his hands and his boots. He had no idea what to say. All he could think of was "Its okay. It's all over. Rest. Help will be here soon." Some of them had already died. Help would be too late for many of them.

Rapowski ran up to him. "It's the truck. They must have hit a mine. They're all dead. Everyone."

"Found the radio, Max," Santori said. "They call this place Buchenwald."

Max looked down and saw raindrops on his hands. The sun was shining. It wasn't raindrops. It was teardrops—Max's tears.

# Chapter One

New Rochelle, New York, 1949

"Good morning. Chambers Investigation Services. How may I help you?"

"Uhh, I lost my dog last night. D'ya think you could find him?" said the husky voice on the phone.

"Oh, Max, you'll have to come up with something better than that," said Sally.

"Good morning, kid," said Max. "Any appointments today?"

"Yes!" she exclaimed. "A man called just as I was closing up last night. He said it was a 'matter of utmost importance that he sees you as soon as possible,' so he'll be here at nine."

"What does he want?"

"He wouldn't tell me. He said he could only speak with you, for 'security purposes.' He had a foreign accent."

"Okay, I'm leaving now. Be sure to drink all your milk."

"Ha ha, Mr. Funny Bones."

Max always kidded his secretary, Sally Connors. She was twenty-three years old and looked about ten years younger. This was her first job. She was cute as a button and American as apple pie. When Max's mother met her, she said in her native Italian, "Signorina Panebianco." Ms. White Bread! She meant it in the nicest possible way.

Max sat at the kitchen table and lit a cigarette, while his wife, Carol, poured the coffee. She made great coffee, almost as strong as espresso. She was a hell of a good cook, and she was a knockout to boot. She had long black hair, blue eyes, legs like Betty Grable, and built like Ann Sheridan. They met in London on V-J Day. She was a WAC, and he was drunk. It was love at first sight as they say. They were married after a month. God, he loved her.

"W-would you like some eggs, Max?" Carol asked. She had an adorable stammer. Max thought so, but she was very self-conscious about it. She was usually very quiet, and Max had to drag a conversation out of her.

"No, thanks, honey," he said. "I actually have an appointment this morning. Can you believe it?"

"Th-that is great! I know you w-will do w-well."

"Well, let's hope so. I'll see you later. Gimme a kiss, gorgeous." They kissed passionately.

"Th-that is for luck," she said.

"I'll need it, babe."

He checked himself in the mirror by the door. His brown hair was slicked back, a little long but not yet bushy. There was a little gray at his temples, which made him look a bit older than his thirty-one years. *It could only help my image,* he thought.

He rubbed his hand over his strong chin, a nice, clean shave. It always looked like he needed a shave, even now, half an hour later. He could probably grow a nice beard; in fact, he had one during the war. Most guys did in one form or another. But it wouldn't be good for a private eye. You'd have to be unobtrusive, blend into the scenery.

He put on his fedora and squared his shoulders. He was five-foot-ten but looked a bit taller. His blue eyes and perfect nose betrayed his Italian ancestry. He always liked his profile. He thought he looked a little like Robert Taylor. His sister Julie said he looked more like Jerry Lewis.

# Chapter Two

**M**ax and Carol lived with his folks when they first got back from the war. He thought it was fun with both of them squeezed into his small bed in his old room. They had to be quieter than a mouse pissing on cotton when they made love. His parents were in the next room, and Max knew that Mama was keeping an ear out for every little sound. He knew that they couldn't stay there for long. It wasn't fair to Carol. She and Max were still trying to get used to each other, and it wasn't any easier to be under the watchful eyes and ears of his parents, eager to pick up anything to gossip about. Not so much Papa, but Mama lived to gossip.

After about three months, Max returned from a long and fruitless day of job searching. Papa asked him to come down to the cellar. Max thought he was needed to help with the wine that Papa was always fiddling with. Three great barrels were full of fermenting wine, and cases of bottled wine were stacked against one wall. Papa motioned Max to pull up a stool to the long wooden workbench that took up another wall. It was packed with tools and gadgets that always intrigued Max when he was a boy. This was where they spoke of important matters that weren't meant for Mama's ears. It was where Max told his father about his draft notice. It was where Papa told sixteen-year-old Max about the birds and the bees. That was a short conversation. Papa rushed through a rehearsed speech that was nothing that Max hadn't already learned from his friends, but he appreciated the thought.

Papa lit his pipe. Max loved to watch him clean and pack the pipe with that wonderful-smelling tobacco. He started smoking a pipe to emulate Papa. He felt so grown-up when he lit it and casually blew the smoke out of the side of his mouth. Mama nearly fell over the first time she saw Max smoke. His sisters, Julie and Dottie, called him grandpa when he smoked the pipe in front of them. They had been sneaking cigarettes for a while, but Max was the first to do so openly. Papa merely shook his head and said that it was a terrible habit to start, and it probably wasn't very healthy.

As they sat, Papa gently placed his hand over Max's.

"Maxie," he said in his broken English, "your mother and I worried so much when you were in the army. A lot of boys no come home. We see the gold stars in the windows. A lot of boys come back like a *senza niente* up here." He tapped his temple, meaning that they had mental problems. "We pray every day that-a you come home safe. Now we thank God every day."

"Thanks, Pop. We all prayed over there too. I guess we got through to the Big Guy."

"So now you come home, and you bring a big surprise with you. You now a married man. What are you gonna do?"

"Well, I tried for a job with the police here in New Rochelle. I tried to get a job as a state trooper. I applied with the Larchmont Police, Mamaroneck Police, and the Mount Vernon Police. They don't want Italians. I don't know how, but as soon as they find out I'm Italian . . . nothing. They're all Irish, and that's all they want. I put in an application to the New York City Police, but I don't think that's going to work out any better."

"So what are you gonna do?"

"I've got an idea that I could get a license to be a private investigator and open up my own office. You know, they sneak around and catch a husband cheating on his wife or find a missing person, stuff like that."

"So what are you gonna do?"

Max smiled. He knew what Papa was doing. He didn't have to say much, but he put it in a way that made you figure out a problem on your own.

"Well, 'what I'm gonna do' is get my private investigator license. Then I'm going to get any job that I can find and save up enough money to open an office. I think I'd be a good private investigator."

"I think so too. What job you gonna get? Dig a ditch, drive a truck, be a garbageman?"

"I don't know, Pop. There are a lot of guys out there looking for jobs. It's tough."

"I know. I work in the factory for thirty years. I saved my money for this house. I gotta no mortgage."

Papa Chambers actually worked for thirty-two years in a factory that made cameras. He worked his way up to inspector, checking all the cameras that didn't pass quality control. It was a tedious job that required knowledge and patience, but he was glad to have it. He stayed employed through the Great Depression when many men were selling apples and standing in breadlines. Now he had a pension and Social Security.

He reached into his breast pocket and took out a small passbook and put it in Max's hand.

"What's this?"

"I saved my money. I saved your money that you sent home from the army. I saved it for you."

Max opened the passbook and flipped through the pages. He saw small deposits made regularly for years. On the final page was the balance of $3,680.63.

"Pop, I can't take this. This must be all your savings."

"No, I saved this just for you. Your sisters both got good husbands. They gonna be taken care of. You lost three years in the war, and now you got a wife to take care of. You gotta be the man of the house now. My papa helped me come to America. Now I help my boy who fights for America. Buy a house, buy your office, and start a family. Me and Mama want to see your kids."

Tears came to Max's eyes. That wasn't anything new. He cried at good card tricks. It was the Italian blood that coursed through his veins that made him so emotional. He looked over and saw that Papa was crying too. They hugged each other for a long while. Max kissed his father's grizzled cheek and got a kiss in return.

"Thank you, Papa. I'm going to go give Mama a big kiss."

Wiping his eyes with a handkerchief, Papa said, "Don't tell your sisters. This is for you. What I give to them is not your business either."

When his parents came over from Italy in 1918, they experienced the bigotry and prejudice that most immigrants had to deal with. Unlike most of the immigrants of the time, they actually had a little money with which to start. Max's grandfather had given his son enough so that he wouldn't have to starve and enough to live on until he found a job. So Luigi and Francesca Ciamberi became Louis and Frances Chambers. His sisters, Giulia and Dorotea, became Julie and Dorothy. And thankfully, Massimo became Max. They were all born in the United States, and their parents insisted on speaking English at all times. Unless they lost their tempers, then all bets were off. His parents became U.S. citizens and went to night school to learn English. Papa learned the language and spoke it well. Mama's English, however, was atrocious. She would add an "et" at the end of certain words. So if Max drank too much, Mama would call him drunkenet. Max kidded her that she accidentally signed up for pidgin English.

Both Mama and Papa Chambers looked like the stereotypical Italians whom people saw on the movie screens. Papa was not very tall and had a strong stocky frame. He was not very outgoing and said little unless he was speaking to family or close friends. He originally sported a handlebar mustache but shaved it off when his friends told him about the "Mustache Pete" mafioso and his gang. Louis Chambers was going to be an American, at least on the outside.

Mama Chambers was an entirely different story. Like her husband, she was short and had a sturdy frame. Most days found her cooking huge Italian meals and stirring an ever-present pot of tomato sauce on her stove. Unlike her husband, she was outgoing and outspoken. She had a perpetual scowl on her face, which belied the fact that she had an easy laugh and a good sense of humor. She also had very thin skin and angered easily when she thought she was being made fun of. Max and his sisters continuously made fun of her English, and she would chase them with a wooden spoon to dole out punishment. She also cursed like a drunken sailor, partly because it was her second language, and she didn't fully understand the severity of the profanity. Deep down, she enjoyed the attention.

The money from his parents was enough for a large down payment in his house and enough to open and set up his office. Max was able to rent a space in the Kaufman Building. He was so proud of his office. He hired a secretary, the first girl who showed up. She was a cute kid and looked a bit like Virginia Mayo. Earnest, eager, and early, that was Sally Connors. She had lost her father and elder brother in the war. She was nineteen at the time but looked fourteen. She was helping support her mother and two younger sisters. Max felt sorry for her and offered her a salary of $60 a week. It was more than he could afford, but he knew it was for a good cause. Sally's mom took in sewing and needed her to help with the bills.

They had a small party the first day Max opened the office. Mom and Pop were there. Julie and Eddie; Dottie and Gus; Sally's mom, Maureen; and her two sisters, Katherine and Annamarie, were there too. Papa brought his best wine, and Mama cooked up a feast of eggplant parmigiana, baked ziti, and zeppole with anchovies. The Irish Connors had never seen such food. Max could tell that they were wary of it and politely took small portions. After tasting it, they went back for more. Mama sent all the leftovers home with them. Sally was Signorina Panebianco and her family was La Familia Panebianco according to Mama. She meant it in the nicest possible way. No calls came to the office, which was good because Max and almost everyone else were drunk by noon. Max even invited the CPA John L. Woodson in the office next door to the party.

The drive to his office was only about fifteen minutes. He drove a 1939 Model A Ford convertible. His pal, Gino, helped him with the engine and a beautiful paint job. Max insisted on dark blue. Gino suggested bright red, but Max said that it needed to be unobtrusive. He was a private eye after all. Bright red would be noticed a mile away.

In fact, it had already helped him with his last job. It seemed someone had painted swastikas on the Beth El Temple in town. His buddy, Phil Green, and his family went there. Max was happy to help. After the war, one of the things that really burned him up was anti-Semitism. He sat in his unobtrusive car for two nights with a thermos of coffee and cigarettes. They showed up on the second night, three kids and a can of paint. Max sneaked up on them just as they were about to start painting. He pulled out his gun with no intention of using it but was sure he would scare the shit out of them.

"Drop the can and put your hands in the air!" he yelled.

"C'mon, Officer," said the mouth, "we were just havin' some fun!"

"Fun?" Max asked. "Fun? How would you like Nazis painting shit on your churches, houses, stores?" He slapped the mouth hard across the face. "I'm no cop, so I could shoot you right now and go home and sleep like a baby, you little punk!" He slapped him again, and the kid started to cry. The other two had already started crying.

The police showed up and took the punks away. They went to juvenile court and got a slap on the wrist. But Max got a nice write-up in the local newspaper. He even got a reward on top of his usual $25-a-day fee plus expenses—$300. It was $300! He almost felt guilty accepting it, but the rabbi insisted on it. Not only did it keep his mortgage current, but it also enabled him to keep his office rent and expenses out of the red. When Sally found out, she said, "Yippee! I can get paid now!" With a huge smile, Max told her to "can it" or it'd be her last payday. She was such a cute kid.

As he pulled out of the driveway, Max couldn't help admiring his house. It was a two-story, white with blue trim wrapped around six large rooms. That was three more rooms than where his parents raised a family in. And he always mentioned that it was next door to where Lou Gehrig lived for a while. The street, Meadow Lane, was right out of an Andy Hardy movie—beautiful homes, shade trees, and sculpted landscapes. It always calmed him down to do his yard work, almost hypnotic. Max didn't even mind that the neighbors could see him tending his flower garden.

New Rochelle, New York, was alternately known as The Home Town or the Queen City of the Sound. Originally settled by the French Huguenots in 1699, it contained some of the most sought-after and expensive real estate in the country. Because of its proximity to New York City, it was home to many Wall Street power brokers and Broadway and film stars. Susan B. Anthony, William Randolph Hearst, Thomas Paine, W. C. Fields, Douglas Fairbanks, and Vernon and Irene Castle were among its more famous residents. Eddie Foy and *The Seven Little Foys* donated their property on the corner of Weyman Avenue and Pelham Road to the city where Eddie Foy Park now stands. George M. Cohan wrote the song "Forty-Five Minutes from Broadway" about New Rochelle. Thanhauser Film Studios was located in the west end. Its booming housing market was filling up neighborhoods, such as the affluent Premium Point, Echo Park, Wykagyl, Davenport, and the West End.

"Up the West" was where Max grew up. It was home to most of the Italian population of the city. The Chambers family lived in a small apartment on Second Street. Three rooms for four people were very cramped. That was where Max met his pal, Gino Domenico, whose family lived in the same building. In time, Papa Chambers was able to purchase a beautiful home in the south side of the city on the corner of Liberty Avenue and Elm Street across the street from The College of New Rochelle. He soon filled every square foot of the yard with a vegetable garden.

# Chapter Three

Max pulled into the parking lot of his office building, the Kaufman Building. Located on the corner of North Avenue and Huguenot Street, it was really classy, and it lent an aura of success to his services. He needed it. Plus, it was a great location for when he had to drive to Manhattan or parts of Westchester County. More often than not, he had to dip into his savings to cover the rent, a steep $90 a month. *Who knows,* he thought, *maybe this Bernstein character would be something to cover the rent.*

"Morning, kid," Max said as he entered his office. "How's it going?"

"Hi, Max, can I get you some coffee?"

"That sounds great, Sally. Bernstein didn't cancel on us, did he?"

"No. I've been here since eight thirty. No calls. Ooh, I think that's him at the door! Get behind your desk and look busy," Sally said as she ran to the door.

Max hung up his coat and hat and spread out the newspaper. He thought that would make him seem carefree. *Who needs another client? We're booked solid!*

The intercom buzzed. "Mr. Chambers, Mr. Bernstein is here," Sally said in a very businesslike manner.

"Send him in," Max said in a bored voice. They were really laying it on thick.

"Mr. Chambers, it is a pleasure to meet you. I have heard many good things about you."

He was a little guy, Max thought, maybe five-foot-four, a hundred twenty pounds soaking wet, gray hair, little mustache, and wire framed glasses—very scholarly.

Standing up, Max said as they shook hands, "The pleasure is all mine. Please have a seat. Can I get you anything? Would you like some coffee?"

"If it's no trouble, may I have some tea?" Bernstein said.

"I think we can handle that. Sally," Max said over the intercom, "could you bring Mr. Bernstein some tea, please?"

"I'll bring it right in, sir," she said. Max couldn't hide his smile at the "sir."

"So, Mr. Bernstein, what brings you here today? I was told you had a matter of some importance."

"Yes," he said, "but first, I need to say thank you. You see, we have met before. Do you remember where?"

"Umm, no, I can't seem to. Where was it?"

"Buchenwald. I was one of the residents when you and your comrades liberated the camp," he said. "I was too weak to walk, and you gave me a blanket, told me help was on the way, and you smiled and patted my shoulder. That was the first time I was touched with kindness by someone other than my fellow prisoners in four years. You have no idea how important that small act was to my spirit."

That word—Buchenwald. Max gripped the handle on one of the lower drawers on his desk, out of sight of his guest. It seemed not a day could go by without something to remind him of that horror. He smelled the stench. He knew that it was all in his head, but he smelled that stench just the same, four years and seven thousand miles away from here.

"Well, um"—Max was searching for the words—"I'm happy that you're doing well. I can't imagine what you must have gone through. We saw the results, not the process. So . . . what can I do for you?"

"One more thing," Bernstein said. "We have a mut—"

"Coffee and tea!" Sally burst into the office. Max welcomed the interruption. He hoped the coffee would steady his nerves.

"Thanks, Sally," he said. "I'll let you know if we need anything else. You were saying, Mr. Bernstein?"

"Ah yes, delicious tea. I was saying that we have a mutual acquaintance, Rabbi Silverman from the Beth El Temple. He told me what a good man you are. Well, I said I knew that already from your heroics in the war."

"Oh yes, the rabbi is a nice man," Max said. "I was happy to help them out. It really wasn't any great shakes." The smell. "It was a couple of stupid kids. They made it sound like I was Superman."

"Do not try to minimize what you did. Too many people did nothing in Germany, and that was what made it easy for the Nazis to implement their policies against the Jews. If we had more men like you in Germany, it would have been very different."

Silence. The smell. Awkward silence.

"But let me get down to business as you say here. As you probably know, the Nuremberg trials have been going on for some time now. Goerring, Kietel, Hess, they have been brought to justice. Many of their leaders are still missing. Josef Mengele, Adolph Eichmann, Albert Speer, missing. But through a connection that I have here, I have information that a certain someone is in hiding here in this area. I need your help in bringing this man to justice."

Bernstein leaned back in his chair and sipped his tea—and waited.

Stalling for time, Max lit a cigarette. He offered one to Mr. Bernstein.

"Ah, American cigarettes! Far superior to German. Thank you so much."

More silence. The smell.

With a deep breath, Max waded in. "Why me? I'm sure army intelligence would want this information. They've been doing a good job so far. Why not them?"

"The German people are tiring of all these trials. They want to—how do you say, sweep it under the carpet? They do not want to be reminded of their complicity in the murder of millions of people."

"Be that as it may, the trials are still going on. What makes you think that they won't prosecute this person?"

"He has already gotten away once. Even the great American army does not want the world to know that they let him slip through their fingers."

"Okay, Mr. Bernstein, maybe I can understand that. Why not the FBI?"

"I would not want to involve the FBI, Mr. Chambers. It seems your J. Edgar Hoover does not care for Jews very much."

Scoffing, Max said, "He thinks all Jews are Communists. And he doesn't care for Communists very much. It makes it very convenient. These days they're looking for Commies under every bed. Okay, now I think I understand. What information do you have?"

Smiling, he reached into his beat-up leather briefcase. "By the way, please call me Heinrich. There is no need for formalities. Ah, here it is. The man we are looking for is Karl Schmitt. He was the commandant of Buchenwald."

"Um, Heinrich, the commandant of Buchenwald, was killed the day we liberated the camp. I saw it with my own eyes. Oh, and call me Max."

"Ya, Max. A nice German name. A man wearing the uniform of the commandant was killed. The man you threw to the mob."

Max stiffened in his chair. "So you know. I don't suppose you'll be holding this over my head. War crime. Murder. Does blackmail ring a bell? I think I'll call you Hank?" Max said derisively.

"Ring a bell! I love your sayings here. No, no, no, I am not here to blackmail. I commend you for what you did. I only say that you did it to someone other than Karl Schmitt. Here is the dossier I have compiled on him."

He handed the folder to Max. Paper clipped to the front page was a photo of Karl Schmitt. Max felt a chill when he saw those cold gray eyes filled with hatred and evil.

"But he was on the truck. I put him there myself. There were no survivors," Max said. It was the truck that poor Jimmy Kemp died in.

"We were able to deduce that three of the guards survived. The two Americans were killed, along with nine guards. It was not until over a year later that we were able to account for the guards. Three are missing. One of them is Karl Schmitt."

Max flipped through the folder and found a photo of Schmitt in civilian clothes. He was standing on the deck of a ship. He was talking with two men, but their faces were obscured. The deck was crowded with waving passengers. The name of the ship was visible: *The Valiant.*

"When was this picture taken?"

"*The Valiant* embarked from Antwerp, Belgium, on August 7, 1945. That was the first time it had ever been used for civilian passage. Its destination was London. After that, we lost track of him until this past December. His wife, living in Bremen, was under surveillance. She mailed him a Christmas card."

"A sentimental Nazi! Now I've seen everything!"

"Ja, it is surprising. They did all they could to get to hell, and now they celebrate the birth of Christ. But no matter, we were able to intercept the card and found it was mailed to a post office box in this very city, New Rochelle."

"You know," Max said, "you seem to have it all figured out. You have men taking photos of him on a ship. You have his wife watched. You have his post office box and his love letters. Why don't you have these men stake out the post office? I still don't get why you need me."

"You, my dear man, are one of only a few people who have ever seen this man up close. You could not be more important to the resolution of this case. The men, as you say, are not professionals.

My brother, Wilhelm, took the photo. A fellow survivor of the camps works in the post office. I was watching his wife."

Max continued leafing through the file. He was desperately trying to come up with a reason to say no, but he knew it was useless. Karl Schmitt killed Jimmy Kemp. Max put him on the truck and put Jimmy on the truck. It was his responsibility to make this right, and maybe he'd be able to sleep at night without those terrible nightmares.

"Okay, I'm in," he said resignedly. "My fee is $25 a day plus expenses. If you leave your contact information with my secretary, I'll be in touch with any developments. I don't know how long this may take, could be a while."

"I'll be staying with Rabbi Silverman. He graciously offered to have me stay in his home. You see, he also lost family and friends to the camps. This Holocaust is not strictly a European tragedy. It has worldwide implications that will be felt for generations."

"Uh-huh. I have no doubt about that," Max said, standing. "It's been quite an interesting meeting you, Hank."

Max stuck out his hand, hoping Bernstein would take the hint and leave already, but instead, he slapped an envelope into his outstretched hand.

"I am told a retainer is customary with private investigators. As you said, this may take some time. Some money to cover expenses, you may deduct it from my bill when the time comes."

Max looked in the envelope and counted $500. Bernstein certainly was greasing the wheels.

"This may be a bit too much, Hank, but we'll certainly keep track of everything. I may be poor, but I'm honest."

"Of that I have no doubt, Max. I shall eagerly await any news that you shall have," he said, shaking Max's hand. "Auf wiedersehen."

Bernstein quickly left the office. Max opened the large window behind his desk and breathed in the cold air. He still had the horrid smell of the camp in his nostrils, in his office, in his mind. He knew he was trapped into this business. Oh, Hank had no intention of blackmailing him, sure, and then he played up the guilt Max felt over Jimmy's death. No, now it was murder. He was going to need some help.

"Well, how'd it go?" Sally said, bursting in. "He seemed so happy when he left."

Max tossed her the envelope. "Keep half in the safe and deposit the rest in the bank. I need to get some air. I'll check back in a while, kid," he said while putting on his coat.

"Oh my god, I can't believe he had all this money! What does he want you to do?"

"He wants me to go back in time. See you later."

# Chapter Four

Max took a long drive around town, trying to get a grip on what had just happened. His thoughts soon wandered back to when he first met Carol. It was August 15, 1945, V-J Day, victory in Japan. The war was finally over. Max was in London at the time, and the city was booming with good cheer. Hitler had really tried to destroy London, but the Brits had shown their mettle and carried on with an almost casual confidence. Max liked the British people. They were nothing like they were portrayed in the movies with their "stiff upper lip" and "pip pip, cheerio." They had an energy that was almost contagious. On this night, it seemed that the entire city was trying to tie one on. Max had been to two pubs and was on his way to a third. He was alone, but the places were so crowded and happy that he had great fun. Perfect strangers bought him drinks, a way of saying thanks for his contributions.

The third pub, the Round Table, was just as crowded as the others. Max bumped into Carol as soon as he entered. He had seen her in both of the other pubs, but they were too crowded for him to get close to her. Now standing at the bar, he spotted her again. She was talking with a guy, and they seemed to be pointing at him. Max smiled and winked but soon realized that he was standing in front of the ladies' room. He shook his head and chuckled and ordered a drink. The Brits had great scotch, single malt. It went down like honey. Of course, after about six or seven drinks, anything went down like honey. As he squeezed through the crowd toward the men's room, he bumped into this raven-haired beauty. He made up his mind to buy her a drink when he came out. As he opened the door, he bumped into her again, spilling her drink.

"I think it might be safer for you if I bought you a drink. Whaddaya say?"

"Sure, I would like that."

"I'm Max. How do you do?" he said formally, bowing at the waist.

"I'm Carol. Nice to meet you."

She was wearing a WAC uniform. Max asked her about her outfit and where she had been. She said she didn't want to talk about that stuff. She was sick and tired of the war. Max knew how she felt. He was still trying to come to grips with the horrors he had seen at Buchenwald. Just the thought of it brought back that smell, that awful, ungodly odor.

They had a great time, laughing and singing along when the pub burst into song. The English people loved to sing, and now they had a great reason. Max told Carol his life story. She didn't say much. She was trying to hide her stammer, but that was okay with him. He liked to talk, especially when he'd had a few. He was also thrilled that such a beautiful woman was so interested in him. During the only lull in the conversation, she leaned over and kissed him deeply, oblivious to the crowd.

That night, they made love for the first time. It was an experience that Max had never known. Not the sex; he'd been with other women, but this was nothing he'd ever dreamed of. They were like two wild animals, grunting and groaning and moaning. Max was nuts about her. He was head-over-heels in love with her; it was love at first sight. They spent the next few weeks seeing the sights of London. They saw the medieval castles, Buckingham Palace, and Piccadilly Square. The British had such great names.

After about a month of this bliss, Max asked Carol for her hand in marriage. He was overjoyed that she said yes. He couldn't believe his luck. Maybe he deserved it, he thought, after all he had been through. Sure, that must be it. Someone up there was looking out for him, and this was his reward.

They pooled their meager funds and were able to find two inexpensive wedding bands. They were both Americans, so the wedding wouldn't be a problem. They shopped around for a nice dress; Carol said she wouldn't get married in that uniform, and Max understood. He would wear his dress uniform since he had only worn it once before when his official army photo was taken.

They wound up waking up the only justice of the peace that they could find. He was drunk off his face. His wife was also drunk, and she served as the witness. The justice was so drunk that he said, "You may now kiss my wife!" Max did so after he kissed his bride, and Carol kissed the justice. They were so happy.

Max knew that he was going to catch hell when he got back to the States and Mama found out. She wasn't going to see him walk down the "aisle-et" as she would say. He knew Papa would understand. Men took things differently in these times.

Max literally shook his head to get back to the reality of what had just happened in his office.

Knowing that he would need help, Max decided to ask his pal Gino. They both came from "off the boat" families and dealt with the same bullies and bigots. Gino had a larger family; he was the eldest of seven brothers and sisters. His younger brother Tony had served in the war too. He had taken part in the liberation of the Philippines, among other battles. Next in line was his sister Susie. Her real name was Maria Assunta, and she was engaged to an ex-sailor named Vincent Gugielmo, but he was called Jimmy Williams. No one would ever figure out their names. Gino's other brother was Nicky, a high schooler, who was the sport jock of the family. He was followed by their three sisters—Laura, Florence, and Gloria. Mama Domenico had certainly been kept busy.

He was great with gadgets and a top-shelf auto mechanic. A licensed pilot, Gino and his friend Dick Schwimmer had flown his seaplane around Westchester County one time, and the engine died. The only place to safely land was the county reservoir, and they were lucky to be in the area. Someone had tried that not long before but had hit the fence around it and died. Gino calmly made a beautiful landing, fixed the engine, and returned to the dock. He didn't tell Papa Domenico. Papa thought Gino had a death wish and hated that he flew. Of course, Gino didn't count on the local newspaper to give it a big write-up. Papa woke Gino up, waving his copy of the *Standard Star* and calling him and Schwimmer dumb sons of bitches.

Gino had flown during the war. He made it "over the hump" in Burma several times. The "hump" was part of the Himalayas, where the planes had to fly at a much higher altitude than usual and depended on "dead reckoning," which was flying a certain course for a certain time and hoping you didn't smack into a mountain. The Japanese controlled Burma for most of the war and were fanatical in their defense of their territories. Many planes were shot down going "over the hump," but he'd volunteered when others were wary of making the trek. The first time he made the trip, an experienced pilot told him to "sit on your helmet if you want to keep your balls!" He had flown the B29 flying fortresses and saw a lot of action. Luckily, he never had to confront the horror of the POW camps that the Japs ran. The Japs had their own wartime atrocities.

Gino lived with his family in a large house on the quiet street of Columbus Avenue. His father kept the place in wonderful condition. Neatly trimmed hedges lined the yard, and the grass was mowed perfectly. As Max pulled up along the side of the yard, he heard the roar of engines. Gino had his new plane out in the yard and was revving the engine. He had taken off the wing and tied the tail to a plum tree. Papa Domenico was screaming at Gino while the prop was kicking up clouds of dust, and Mama Domenico was hurriedly taking clothes off the clothesline.

"Bon giorno, Signore Domenico!" Max called out. "Com'e stai?"

The old man cried, "Massimo, si dice un po' di senso a quest' idiota!" Max, talk some sense into this idiot!

"Lui non mai si ascolta niente da nessuno!" He never listens to anyone!

The old man threw his hands in the air and stomped into the house.

Gino crawled out from under the plane covered from head to toe in grease. He was about the same size as Max, maybe a little thinner, with a thick head of reddish-brown hair. He had full lips and an easy, toothy smile. His long thin nose and twinkling light-blue eyes betrayed his full Italian heritage. He moved toward Max with his arms outstretched.

"Hey, Max, give us a hug!" he said with a large smile.

"Not on your life, pal. I see you finally bought that plane. You think she'll ever get off the ground?"

Scoffing, Gino said, "Oh sure! You think I don't know what I'm doing? The guy just wanted to get rid of it. He charged me $175 bucks! All it needed was a $9 part!"

"I don't know how you do it," Max said, shaking his head. "You sure know how to find a bargain. I guess it helps to be cheap."

"Cheap? I'm extremely careful with a buck. I think they call it frugal," he said with a grin.

"Are you still working at that factory down the street?"

"No, I'm trying to become independently wealthy, and they were holding me back," he said with a laugh.

"Say, Gino, let's go in the garage for a minute. I need to talk to you about something. Could you kill the engine?"

"Yeah, sure. Gimme a minute."

"Ciao, signora," Max called out to Mama Domenico. She waved. She was a cute little thing, always puttering around the yard with fruits from the trees wrapped in her apron.

Max looked around the cluttered garage. All sorts of junk filled the little space.

"Jesus, Gino, why don't you get rid of all this junk? You'd be able to park your car in here. I hear that's what garages are for."

"Oh sure, according to you, it's junk. But when you need something, you have to go and buy it. I'll already have it."

"Yup," Max said as he picked a broken Coke bottle, "you'll be the first person I call when I need a broken bottle."

They both laughed.

"All right, I'm sure you didn't come here to talk about this. What's on your mind?"

Max found a seat, and Gino leaned on his workbench. He listened intently as Max told him of his meeting with Hank. He hoped he didn't show how shocked he was at all the horrible details. He tried not to look in Max's eyes, thinking it would be easier to speak of such difficult things without being stared at. He knew Max had been at Buchenwald, but he respected Max's reticence and didn't press him for the gory details. People wouldn't understand the true horror that servicemen faced in the war, so few guys talked about it. He lit a cigarette and let Max finish his story.

"So I'm gonna need some help with this. Think you can find the time?" Max finally said.

"I'll have to check my schedule. The old man is driving me crazy. He wants me to cut the hedges, fix the roof, pick the apples. I start up the engine just to drown him out. But first, let's talk about my compensation and fringe benefits."

"Fringe benefits! I only get $25 a day plus expenses!"

"I'll take it!" Gino said quickly.

"I said I get $25 a day, not you!"

"Whattaya think, I'm just a spaghetti bender? I'm a skilled machinist and a decorated veteran."

"You're decorated with grease right now!" Laughing out loud and shaking his head, he said, "Okay it's a deal."

Max absentmindedly stuck out his hand, and Gino quickly grasped it with a handful of grease.

"Deal, partner!" Gino said with a loud laugh.

Max pulled his hand away, looking for a rag to wipe off the filth. "Be at my office at eight. We'll get to the post office before it opens. And wear some clean clothes!"

"Washing is going to cost extra!" Gino said with a laugh.

Walking back to his car, Max realized that he was smiling. Maybe he'd be able to get a few laughs out of this nightmare.

# Chapter Five

The plan was simple. They would stake out the post office. It was located on the busy corner of Huguenot Street and North Avenue. Max's car was parked facing south and Gino's car facing north. When they made a mark, they would be ready to go in either direction. One man sat inside or on the bench right outside the front doors. The other waited in his car. The signal would have the inside man blow his nose. Then they'd get into whichever car that was pointed in the right direction. It was a good plan, Max thought. The Christmas card had been picked up by the time they had started. The box was empty now. Hopefully, it wouldn't be too long before another piece of mail came in.

The first three days came up empty. Gino was all business once the job started. Max knew he could trust him to be on the ball. He'd buddied up with the postal workers inside and told them he was waiting for a letter addressed to the box. They'd let him know when something came in.

The fourth day was a Tuesday. Sure enough, they let Gino know that a letter came in. They sat in Max's car for a while.

"Stay on the bench outside today," Max said. "We can see the box through the window. It'll be easier to get in the right car."

Nothing happened the rest of the day. No one came to the box. It was tearing Max up inside. He couldn't believe how close he was to finding Karl Schmitt. He wondered if it could really be this easy.

Max invited Gino over for dinner that night. Carol made a delicious beef stew, and they opened a bottle of Papa Chambers's homemade wine. They ate and drank and laughed. Max felt a weight being lifted off his shoulders. It would be just a matter of time before they got this bastard.

Carol was pouring coffee when the doorbell rang. Max was shocked when he opened the door. It was Nicky Kemp, Jimmy's elder brother.

"Nicky! Holy cow!"

"Hi, Max, how have you been? I hope I'm not disturbing you," he said.

"No, not at all. Come in, come in." Shaking his hand, he said, "You know Gino?"

"Oh yeah, hiya, Gino!"

"Hey, Nicky, I haven't seen you in ages. Are you doing okay?" Shaking his hand, Gino said, "How's the family?"

"They're just fine."

"I don't think you ever met my wife. Nicky, this is Carol. Carol, this is Nicky Kemp. His brother, Jimmy, was one of my best friends," Max said.

Carol's eyes widened under her thick glasses as she shook Nicky's hand.

"It is s-s-so nice to m-m-meet you, Jimmy," she said.

"It's Nicky," he corrected.

"Oh m-my god, I am s-s-so sorry!"

"It's all right. Don't let it bother you. It's nice to meet you."

Max noticed that Carol had visibly paled and was starting to shake. He had told her some of what had happened on the day Jimmy died. He didn't say that he put Jimmy on the truck, just that he was killed that day. Gino was the first person to whom he'd told the whole story of that horrible day, so he thought it a little odd that Carol seemed to be so upset. She was always a little nervous when meeting new people and stammered more than usual. *Calling Nicky by his dead brother's name must have thrown her,* Max thought.

"Sit, everyone," Max said. "I'll get another cup, baby. Relax. Gino, tell him about your plane."

"I thought you were racing motorcycles," Nicky said. "What happened?"

"Oh jeez, they were too dangerous for me. My pal Schwimmer nearly drove through a house on North Avenue. I thought planes would be safer."

"The skies will never be friendly again," Max said with a laugh.

"So what brings you here tonight?" Max asked.

"Well, we're bringing Jimmy's remains back from Germany. We're going to put him in the family plot over at the Holy Sepulcher Cemetery. We'd like you to be there, Max. You too, Gino. In fact, we would like you to deliver the eulogy, Max. I hope I'm not putting a damper on your evening."

"We'll be there, all of us. I don't know what I could say though. Couldn't someone in the family . . ." Max trailed off.

"The folks won't be in any condition, but you knew him best. You knew what he was really like. It would really mean a lot," Nicky said.

"If that's the way you feel, I'd be honored."

"I knew you wouldn't let us down, Max. It's probably going to be another month or so. You know the army. They're supposed to let us know when he's on the ship. I'll let you know as soon as we do, okay?"

"That's fine, Nick."

"If you don't mind, I have some more folks to tell." Standing, he shook hands all around. He said with a sad smile, "You guys made me think of the old days for a bit. Good night."

Max leaned against the door. He looked over to Carol and Gino.

"Sure," he said with a forced smile, "I couldn't let them down."

# Chapter Six

**N**eedless to say the evening ended on a somber note. Max and Carol quickly cleaned up and headed upstairs to bed. As he sat in the bedroom armchair, pulling on a cigarette, Max thought how crazily things had changed. He had always been a happy guy, cracking crazy jokes and off-the-wall comments. Now he actually found himself brooding. He wasn't sure that Bernstein was on the level. He could turn Max in at any time.

What would happen to Carol if he were sent away, even for a short while? She had come back from the war a mess. Max would hear her crying behind the bathroom door. She didn't want anything to do with her parents who lived in Baltimore. Every time Max suggested a trip or a phone call or even a letter, Carol would give a resounding no and storm off. The most she ever said about them was that they had treated her terribly because of her stammer. She said that they didn't want her rich relatives thinking they had a feeble-minded, drooling, stammering, retarded child in the family. She was locked away in the house when her parents went visiting, and some excuse was made for her absence. She said she practically had to sneak out to join the WACs.

Carol now spent her days reading after doing all the housework. Max did the grocery shopping because he thought it would be stressful for her to have to speak to strangers. She joined in when they did their gardening and raking leaves, and Max thought it did her a world of good. She would be in a calm, relaxed mood for the rest of the night. They usually made love those nights. She was like a totally different person in bed, pulling at his hair, biting, even scratching up his back with her long fingernails. It was a world of difference to Max's previous experiences with the opposite sex. Sure he had his fumbling moments with girls, but Carol was the real thing.

That was where Max's thoughts were when Carol came out of the bathroom in her pajamas. As she came over to steal a puff off his cigarette, Max pulled her onto his lap and kissed her deeply.

"Not tonight, Max," she said as she pulled away. "I am a-all h-hairy and gross."

Carol regularly shaved her legs stubble-free. She even shaved her pubic area. She said she felt cleaner like that. Max didn't mind. He'd heard of women doing that but never seen it till Carol.

"Who says you're gross?" Max asked. "You're a knockout, and you're driving me crazy. C'mon, babe."

"Does t-t-this drive you crazy?" she asked as she took off her pajama top, exposing her round firm breasts.

"Now you got the right idea."

"W-well, maybe w-we can just w-work on you tonight," she said as she started pulling off his bottoms. "I do not w-want to disappoint you."

She took off her glasses and turned off the light.

# Chapter Seven

Sundays usually found the Chambers clan gathered at Mama and Papa's house for dinner. As soon as she got back from services at the Blessed Sacrament Church, Mama started cooking the tomato sauce. There was always an argument about whether to call it gravy or sauce, but it always came out fantastic. In fact, Mama made the sauce in bulk. A man with a truck would come by every once in a while with bushels of different fresh vegetables from the Hunts Point Market. When he had tomatoes, Mama would buy twenty to thirty bushels and start making sauce. She would cut and cook them and then run them through a straining machine with a crank handle that pulled out all the seeds and skins. Then she would fill bottles or mason jars with the sauce. It was a long procedure, and Mama worked like a dog getting it done. There was an old wives' tale that if any of the women helping out was having her period, the sauce would spoil. Therefore, Julie and Dottie inevitably had their periods when Mama started her project. Mama always had a cousin or niece to help her out. Her house was filled with the tomatoes and all the remnants of the process. And there was always a mad search for more bottles and jars. Mama would kill if she found that someone had thrown out something that could be used for the sauce. When she gave a bottle or jar to someone, she would say, "This is-s a called return-et," meaning she wanted the jar back. Carol was never asked to help out. She and Mama had never gotten close.

Today dinner was eggplant parmigiana, Max's favorite, and ziti with meatballs, sausages, and *bracciole*. Everyone ate well, "like-a you just got out of-a jail" as Mama liked to say. Max filled up; Carol just couldn't make Italian food that came close to Mama's. Papa filled everyone's glasses with his homemade wine whether they wanted it or not. "Drink, it's good-a for you," he would say. Between the strong wine and it being the middle of the afternoon, the ladies had a nice buzz. There was a lot of laughter and yelling. The yelling was just a way of life. It wasn't done with malice; one had to yell to be heard over the din. All the children would come running through the dining room once they were finished with their meals in the kitchen. The dining room was for the adults.

After the dinner dishes were done, coffee and dessert were served. Mama made her espresso nice and strong. One cup would clear the head of any drunk in minutes. Today the dessert was pastries. A large platter was filled with cannoli, *sfogliatelle*, and assorted Italian cookies.

The next few days dragged. No one came to open box 714. On Friday morning, Max had a brainstorm.

"Keep an eye out, Gino. I've got to get to a phone."

He was back in a minute and told Gino the plan.

At 4:30 p.m., Sally Connors strolled up to the car. She was wearing one of her mother's old housedresses and no makeup, except a dark circle under her left eye.

"All set, boss," she said excitedly.

"Great," he said. "You look the part."

"Slap me."

"What?"

"Slap me. I've got to get into character."

"Can't you just pretend?"

"It's called method acting, silly. Montgomery Clift and John Garfield do it."

"Montgomery who?" Gino asked.

"Clift! Don't you go to the movies?"

Before Gino could answer, Max gave her a hard slap across the face.

"Is that what you're looking for?" he asked.

"Wow," she said, rubbing her face. "I'm suffering for my art."

At 4:45 p.m., Sally entered the post office with a handkerchief to her face, sobbing loudly. She sat at the PO box desk.

"What seems to be the problem, young lady?" asked the surprised clerk.

"I lost the key to our box," she said between sobs. "My husband will kill me!"

"We'll have to open a new box. It won't take long."

"NO! Then he'll know! I'm sure I can find the key. I just need to get the letter in there."

"Well . . . all right. What is your name and box number?"

Sally purposely mumbled incoherently but clearly said, "Box 714."

The clerk asked again, and Sally started crying loudly, attracting the attention of the manager.

"Lew," said the manager, "open this lady's box right now. Can't you see she's in trouble?"

Lew, the clerk, quickly got up and went to the box with Sally.

"There you are, Mrs. Wagner," he said, handing her the letter. "If you ever need anything else, you come see me, Lew Prest."

"Oh, thank you,' Sally said between sobs. "Thank you so much!"

As Sally walked to Max's car, Gino went inside and literally leaned on box 714 until the post office closed at five o'clock.

Handing Max the letter, she said, "Piece of cake. You should have called for my help sooner."

"You are a peach, kid!"

# Chapter Eight

They all went right over to Max's house to inspect the letter. It was postmarked in Cleveland, Ohio. Max steamed it open over the teakettle. It was a cipher, written in a code.

"Say," Gino said, "I've got a couple of books on codes. Let me go get them."

"Great," Max said. "Bring some pizza with you. Carol, can you put on some coffee? We may be up for a while."

Realizing that Sally was still there, Max called out to Gino, "Hey, give this kid a ride home."

"Oh no," she said. "I'm in this now, and I'm in it for the long haul, Max."

"Listen, this is not a part of your job."

"I'm staying!"

"Sally, you are my secretary. 'Fieldwork' is not in your job description. Besides, this could get dangerous."

"Without me, you would still be sitting in front of the post office!"

She was right, Max thought, but he couldn't let anything happen to her. Aside from being a remarkable breath of fresh air and full of life, she was supporting her family. Her father and elder brother had been killed in the war, and Sally was helping support her mother and two little sisters.

"Okay, but your wings are clipped. We can use you but only in the research part of the case. I can't have you in the field. Got it?"

"Okay, okay, Mr. Simon Legree. Ummm, I think this deserves overtime pay."

"Oh brother, between Gino's fringe benefits and your overtime, I'll be in the poorhouse in no time at all!"

Gino was back within the hour with the pizza and three books that had some basic code systems. They should have stuck with just the pizza because the books were useless. They couldn't make heads or tails of the code, not with these books. Around midnight, Max decided to call it a night.

"Tomorrow we have some work to do. We'll check the library and any bookstores for some books about codes."

# Chapter Nine

The water at Glen Island beach was absolutely beautiful. It was warmer than Max could ever remember. He trotted across the lush green lawn to his blanket and lay down in the warm sun. It was simply a gorgeous day. As the saltwater dripped off him and his swimsuit, a gentle breeze blew. Max could hear the children playing behind him. A softball game and games of tag and hide-and-seek were going on, and the familiar phrases were shouted.

"You're it!"

"Holy cow, it's a triple!"

"Olly olly oxen free!"

"Billy, throw it to third!"

"Hey, Max, want a ride?"

"You never tagged me! I'm safe!"

"I'm gonna tell on you!"

"Hey, Max, want a ride?"

Max looked around to see whether it was him being called.

"Over here, Max."

Max found the source of the call. It was a familiar figure, giggling. He'd heard that giggle all during his childhood. No one had that high-pitched cackle but Jimmy Kemp. And there he was with his usual shit-eating grin.

"How's the water? I'd join you for a swim, but I'm not dressed for it."

He wasn't dressed for swimming. He was wearing those same muddy boots, the same tattered fatigues, and that same helmet tilted to the side, leaning on that same Nazi truck that Max ordered him to take.

"Jimmy, get out of here before the kids see you and that truck!"

"What kids? Take a look around, pal."

The kids were all gone. Gone also was the lush green field. In its place was mud—thick black mud, barbed wire, and dingy gray buildings that housed the poor souls of Buchenwald. He was back, back in that camp of horrors, back to that terrible day, back to that familiar stench—again.

"Jimmy, why do you keep doing this to me? It was war! I didn't know what was gonna happen. We'd just gone down that road, and there were no mines. I wouldn't have sent you if I'd known. It's not my fault!"

"Sure it is, pal. You wanted to get me out of there before all the brass showed up, take all the credit for yourself."

"Credit for what? Four men were killed. One man was with a nervous breakdown. Who the fuck wants credit for that? I didn't know what was gonna happen!"

"You knew, pal. You knew."

"Jimmy, just go away."

"Go away? I'm coming back, pal. Did you forget? You're doing the eulogy, pal. Are you gonna tell all about me? About what you did? You never told my folks what happened. What was it you said? Oh yeah, 'Jimmy was killed in an explosion. He never knew what hit him.' You didn't say I was blown to pieces. You didn't tell them that I was roasted in the fire. You didn't tell them that I was a bundle of charbroiled body parts. My own mother wouldn't have recognized me. All because of you. Why don't you say that in your fucking eulogy?"

"I didn't know what was gonna happen. I DIDN'T KNOW WHAT WAS GONNA HAPPEN!"

Max looked in the cab of the truck and saw them. He saw Lew Frazier. Frazier was staring ahead, but the guy in the middle looked back at Max. He had those same cold gray eyes filled with hatred. Karl Schmitt in the flesh.

Now he wore a thin smile. He was smiling because he made it out of the truck alive, he and two other prisoners. How did he do it? How did they do it? Did they kill Jimmy and Frazier, the rest of the prisoners, and then blow up the truck? He looked into Max's eyes.

"*Auf wiedersehen,* Jew lover."

"Jimmy, don't get in the truck. I'm sorry for what I said. Stay out of the truck. Frazier, get out of there. Get out!"

"Hey, make up your mind, pal. Oh, by the way, say hi to your pretty wife, Max. She's got nice tits."

"Don't get in the truck, Jimmy!"

Max tried to stop him, but he was stuck in that mud. He sunk knee-deep in that stinking mud. He started crawling, pulling away handfuls of mud in front of him, but he couldn't pull himself one inch closer to the truck. He looked on helplessly as Jimmy climbed into the driver's seat and started the engine.

"See you soon, pal. Don't forget to write your speech."

"Stop! Stop, Jimmy! Don't go down that road! Get out of the fucking truck! GET OUT OF THE FUCKING TRUCK! I DIDN'T KNOW! I DIDN'T KNOW!"

"Wake up, Max. Honey, you are dreaming."

Max woke. He was dripping with sweat and tangled in his bedsheets. Tears were streaming down his face, and he was holding back sobs.

"I'm sorry, babe. I didn't mean to wake you. Just a stupid dream."

"That's all right, Max. I understand."

She pulled him back down on the bed and mopped his brow and stroked his hair.

"I understand everything."

# Chapter Ten

I t all happened so fast, too fast to follow any prearranged plan. Where did they go wrong? Things went wrong from the first step, and no matter what they did, things only got worse.

Max, Gino, and Sally waited in Gino's car for the post office to open. It was Monday morning, and the street was slowly coming to life. They watched as one of the postal workers unlocked the front door and let in the two old ladies who were waiting outside. They could see box 714 from the car, and the coast was clear.

Sally crossed the street, wearing the same battered-wife outfit she wore when she got them to open the box. She reached up her hand to drop in the letter. Suddenly, a huge hairy paw grabbed her tiny wrist.

"What do you think you are doing, *fräulein*?" asked the owner of the paw in a heavy German accent.

"Oh, oh, I was just putting this in the box. I found it on the floor."

"Shut up! Do you think I am stupid?"

"Let me go! I'll call for the police!"

"You will be dead before you open your mouth," he hissed in her ear.

She felt the gun in her ribs before she looked down to see it.

"Come with me, you little bitch!"

Max and Gino watched in horror as Sally walked out the door held tightly by a large man.

"Gino, where the fuck did he come from?"

"I don't know. No one went in after she did. He must have been in there already!"

The big man shoved Sally into his convertible. He put the gun on his lap but had a vice grip on her wrist. He pulled out into traffic and headed south on North Avenue.

"Stay on his ass, Gino. We can't lose him with Sally!"

"He ain't getting away!"

The car turned left onto Main Street, and three cars got between them.

"That's far enough. Don't lose them!

"Relax, Max. On him like a cheap suit!"

"Now I'm relaxed. You'd know all about cheap suits. Look, he's turning right on Franklin. I bet he thinks he lost us. He's not even speeding."

A smile crossed the German's face as he checked his rearview mirror.

"I seem to have lost your comrades. Now you and I can have a little talk. What was in the letter?"

"I don't know what you're talking about! Let me go!"

He twisted her arm until she cried out in pain.

"I know you are lying. Do it again and I will break that little arm of yours. What was in the letter?"

"I-I don't know. It was a code. They couldn't figure it out!"

That seemed to satisfy him as he eased his grip on Sally's arm.

"Very good. Now where is the Jew?"

"Who are you talking about?"

"You know who I mean! Bernstein! Where is he?!?"

"I-I don't know. He never told us where he was staying."

They had to stop for a red light at the corner of Franklin and Pelham Road. Max saw this as his only chance. Crouching low, he got out of the passenger door.

"If I don't get them, run 'em off the fucking road," Max said as he started toward the light.

"You got it!"

Max was running, bent over like an old man. He had to get there before the light turned green, or he'd blow the chance. The light changed as Max was one car behind, and he watched as they started turning right on Pelham Road. Running over the lawn of the corner house, he saw Sally's head turn. Their eyes met, and she knew what Max was trying to do. She bent over and bit the German's hand as hard as she could.

"Ahh! You bitch!" the German screamed and pulled his hand away.

As he raised his arm to backhand Sally, Max was in the air. Using a park bench as a springboard, he flew into the open car's back seat, smacking the side of the German's head before he landed. The car swerved violently, knocking Max down as he was starting to get his footing. Steadying himself, he put a chokehold on the German with both arms.

"Get out, Sally! Open the door and jump!"

Hearing this, the German pressed the gas pedal to the floor while still swerving all over. Max was squeezing as hard as he could but couldn't get his elbow under the man's chin. The German stomped on the brake, sending Max over the seat, ramming his head into the dashboard. Max twisted his body till he was upright and felt a jarring blow from the fist of the German.

"Get out, Sally!"

"I can't! He's going too fast!"

Just then, a hand reached over and grabbed the back of Sally's dress. It was Gino, pulled along the passenger side of the car. The cars were scraping together.

"Jump in! I got you! Do it now!"

Taking a deep breath, Sally got her feet onto the seat and leaped into the car. Her head landed on Gino's lap, her knee striking his jaw and her left arm through the steering wheel, causing him to bounce off a couple of parked cars. Her legs were kicking wildly in the air, kneeing Gino's face with every other kick.

"Sally, stop moving! You're gonna kill us! I got you! Just stay still!"

She went limp, and Gino was able to pull over to a stop. Her dress was bunched up around her waist, and her legs were bent over the driver's side door with her head on Gino's lap.

"If we were on a date, I'd say it was going well. Are you okay, kid?"

"Will you help me get my head out of your crotch?!"

"I never heard that before. Okay, get your arm out. Sit up. How do you feel? Are you all right?"

"I lost a shoe!"

"I guess that's a yes. Hold on. We've got to catch up to them."

Max and the German were trading blows while swerving down Pelham Road. *He's too strong for me,* Max thought. Max would land a punch on his jaw, and his head would barely turn. When the German landed one, it sent Max onto the floor mats. *Wrestle him,* Max thought. *He's got to keep one hand on the wheel.* He was able to get his arm around the German's neck and punched him square in the nose twice. The car was speeding along at 60 mph, amazingly avoiding any oncoming traffic. Max hit him again. He knew he was hurting the larger man.

"Where is Karl Schmitt?!" Punch. "Who are you?!" Punch. "Where is Karl Schmitt?!"

Max broke his grip when he felt a bolt of lightning hit him in the belly. The German raised his arm and rammed his elbow into Max's groin again. As he crumpled in the seat, the large man grabbed a handful of hair and rammed Max's head into the dashboard. He did it again, and Max lost consciousness. He shoved Max back down to the floorboards.

The German looked around and checked his bearings. He needed to get to Glen Island Marina. He relaxed a bit when he realized he hadn't missed the turn; it was just ahead. Wiping the blood from his nose, he spat out a mouthful at Max's unmoving body. The left turn was made at a leisurely pace as the German smiled at the thought of drowning Max before he took off in his boat.

*Americans.* He scoffed. *Pampered and weak. We would have beaten them if not for the Russians. The only mistake the Führer made was to take them both on at the same time. If only we had—* The thought was interrupted by a blast in his face.

Max had come to on the floor of the car. It seemed he'd closed his eyes for only a few seconds, and then he realized he was knocked out. Careful not to move, he took a few deep breaths. He had to move. He couldn't let this bastard hit him again, not like this. The son of a bitch just spat on him. He felt his right foot was planted against the door. Bracing himself, he struck.

The backhand hit the German flat on the nose, and Max felt the bones break. He followed with a roundhouse right to the same spot. Seizing the moment, Max jumped and got his arm around the German's throat, squeezing as hard as he could. Choking, the large man floored the gas while pulling at the arm around his neck. Max positioned his leg to keep from getting hit in the balls again and saw the speedometer rising—40 mph, 50 mph, 60 mph. He had to do something before this guy killed them both.

The German broke Max's grip on his throat. *Holy shit!* Max thought. *It's like fighting a tree trunk! But the tree trunk has a broken nose. Keep hitting him there.* And he did. Again and again, he hit him until his nose was just a bloody pulp hanging to one side of his face. But trouble lay ahead. Bells were ringing.

They were heading toward the bridge, the drawbridge. And the bridge was up. The car splintered the wooden barrier, going ninety miles per hour, and up they went. Max tried to get his foot on the brake, but the German threw him aside like a rag doll. The bridge was actually on its way down. *We might have a chance,* Max thought. Off they went, but they didn't have a chance.

The car actually hit the other side of the bridge. It crashed into the edge of the other side, about four feet under the roadway. The German's head bounced off the steering wheel, while Max hit a familiar spot on the dashboard. It rolled over to the right and headed nose down to the dark water below. It landed with a loud splash, and then there was quiet.

The cold water surrounding Max was like a slap in the face. He'd been thrown clear when the car rolled over and took a long plunge on his own. He floated in place for a bit, couldn't see a thing. *Nope,* he thought, *I'm not dead. I'm in too much pain. When you're dead, there are supposed to be harps and angels.* The ice-cold water felt like a million needles in his skin. *Enough of this. Let me get out of here. Kick. Kick, you son of a bitch! Now I need some air. I really need some air! Shit, I need some air! Kick.* KICK! KICK!

Max broke the surface of the water, gasping loudly for air. The water was freezing, and he knew he had to make to the shore quickly. He was a good swimmer, but he hurt all over. He couldn't see the car or the German. He paddled around, looking for something. It was hard to get a good look from his level in the water. Then he saw the bubbles about twenty feet away. Swimming a few strokes, he got to the point and dove. It was easy. The bubbles were like little light bulbs that led to the car. And the German, he was dead. Max checked his jacket for a wallet, for some ID. Nothing. Air running out, he checked one more pocket and found the letter. He took it, and up he went.

As he broke through the surface, he heard sirens. He couldn't be sure which they were—police, ambulance, or fire department. They would all be here soon enough. He started swimming toward the shore. What story would he tell? What happened with Sally and Gino? It didn't take long to find out.

"Hey, get out of the water, you stupid bastard. Don't you know it's too cold for swimming?" Gino called out from the shore.

"Hurry up, Max! You're going to freeze like those people on the *Titanic!*" Sally cried out.

They pulled him the last few feet out of the water.

"Here comes the police. Don't tell them anything until you talk to me. Pretend to be unconscious."

"Gino, I won't be pretending."

With that, Max closed his eyes.

# Chapter Eleven

Karl Schmitt nervously paced the front room of his small Queens apartment overlooking the Union Turnpike. He hadn't heard from Hans or his other partner in hours. It was supposed to be a quick "snatch job," followed by a boat trip to the New Jersey shore. Something must have happened, he thought, as they were all very precise with their instructions. It was the German way.

The door opened, and in walked his other partner, Tom Dekerry, dressed the same as Karl in the garb of a Hasidic Jew.

"Have you heard from Hans?" Karl asked. "He should have checked in hours ago."

"Even better," Tom said as he flopped into an old overstuffed chair. "I read about him." Tossing a copy of the *Standard Star*, the local New Rochelle paper, on the coffee table, he said, "He's dead. Read it and weep."

"Do you expect me to translate that into German? Just tell me what happened!"

"Well, my Kraut friend, Chambers was able to save the girl, and they wound up driving off the bridge at Glen Island. Hans drowned, and Chambers is in New Rochelle Hospital right now. They don't say much about his condition. With a little luck, he will die from his injuries. If I know Hans, he probably gave him a hell of a beating."

"*Mein Gott!* You said it would work like a 'charm,' you fool!"

"Ease up there, *heine*. These things happen, and besides, they have the letter."

"That letter had better work."

"It will work, believe me. Let's look on the bright side. Our piece of the pie just got bigger."

Schmitt thought for a minute, and a thin smile crossed his bearded face.

"Ja, it did get bigger. *Auf wiedersehen*, Hans. Thank you for your service to the fatherland."

"Fatherland, my ass! We're in the United States now."


"Don't get in the truck, Jimmy! Don't get in the truck!"

"Mr. Chambers."

"Don't get in the truck—"

"MR. CHAMBERS! WAKE UP!"

Max opened his eyes. He looked at a hideous face and couldn't contain a scream.

"AAHH!"

"You were dreaming, Mr. Chambers."

The voice came from the ugliest face he had ever seen. It was six or seven inches from his face, and he jumped in fright.

"You're in the hospital, Mr. Chambers. You were injured trying to save a man at Glen Island."

"Who the hell are you?"

"I'm Nurse Adious."

She was truly repulsive. Her narrow eyes were topped by long gray eyebrows, and her thin-lipped mouth was in a permanent frown. Her long nose had graying hair growing out of her nostrils, and her skin was the pallor of old newspaper.

"You have some visitors outside. Do you feel up to some company?"

"Oh, um, yeah, but I have to use the bathroom first."

"I'll get you a pan."

"I don't need a bedpan. I'm perfectly capable of peeing into a toilet, by myself."

"I'll give you a few minutes."

Max got out of bed on unsteady feet. He didn't remember coming to the hospital and wasn't sure how long he'd been asleep. He leaned a hand on the wall as he urinated. It seemed to go on forever, and he was getting light-headed just as he finished. He climbed back in to the warm bed and pulled up the covers just as the door opened.

"Massimo, Massimo," cried Mama Chambers as she hugged him tightly as only a mother could. "We were so worried for you. I was a-terrified. I brought you a prosciutto sandwich."

"I'm fine, Mama."

Papa Chambers bent over the other side of the bed and gave Max a kiss on the forehead.

"Dio mio, Massimo! Che cazzo stai facendo?" Goddammit, Massimo! What the fuck have you been doing?

Max shrugged. "It's okay, Pop. Everything is under control."

"Eh, sure, niente sta buono!" Nothing is okay!

But Papa Chambers had a relieved smile on his face. He knew Max was lying, probably to keep him from worrying.

His sisters came running in with their husbands. Julie and Eddie stood next to Papa and Dottie and Gus next to Mama, who was crying tears of joy. Eddie pulled out his trusty flask and handed it to Max.

"Drink up, buddy. You deserve it!"

Max quickly grabbed it and took a long pull. He knew Mama would take it away, and she did so quickly.

"Eddie, he's-a sick. Why you gotta give-a him a-that?"

"Mama, he's a hero! He deserves it! He nearly died trying to save that jerk who drove off the bridge."

"Well, I'm not sick. Let me have some of that," said Gus.

Max looked around. "Where is Carol? Is she here?"

Julie answered, "She just went out to get us some coffee with Gino. They should be back any minute."

"Oh god, I could use a cup of coffee. How long have I been here?"

"It is now Wednesday afternoon," said Dottie. "You've been out for over two days. The doctor said you have a concussion."

"Hey, get out of that bed, you lazy bastard!" cried Gino as he entered the room with Carol.

She brushed past everyone and gave Max a tearful hug. She didn't say anything, but she was sobbing loudly.

Mama stood back and rolled her eyes at what she thought was a spectacle, and the room filled with laughter. She said, "Quanto mostra i cazzo!" What a fucking performance!

The flask was passed around some more, and everyone relaxed.

"Hey, you made the papers, Max," Gino said as he pulled out a copy. "'Local man injured trying to save doomed motorist at Glen Island.' They didn't find any ID on him. They have no idea who he was."

"Is that right?"

"Yeah, Max. It's a good thing we were down there fishing."

"Riiight . . ."

They all laughed and joked with Max for a while. The door opened, and Nurse Adious entered.

"All right," she said, "that will be all for today. Mr. Chambers has suffered a serious injury and needs his rest. Everyone must leave."

Mama said, "Si puo mangiare merda che brutta puttana!" Eat shit, you ugly whore!

"EVERYONE OUT! NOW!"

They all gave Max big hugs and slowly filed out. Carol and Gino were the last ones left in the room.

Gino whispered, "I told the detectives that we were all down at the beach for a little fishing. You jumped in when you saw the car go off the bridge. They believed every word. So don't worry, buddy."

Carol still couldn't speak. Max held her face in his hands and kissed her.

"I'm fine, baby. I just got a little bump on the head. Please don't worry."

"Okay, Max."

"Gino, could you take her home and make sure she's inside safely?"

"Don't worry about a thing, buddy. I'll try to sneak back in later."

As they left, Max leaned back on his pillow. He had a tremendous headache but was glad that he only had a concussion. *They aren't very serious,* he thought and closed his eyes.

The door opened, and in walked a doctor.

"I'm Dr. Churn," said the tall bald man in a monotone. "You've been under my care for the last two days. You have a concussion, nothing too serious. You should be able to go home in a few days."

"Anything I need to worry about, Doc?"

"No, you just have to rest. When you get home, you'll need to rest a bit but no need to worry. I'm leaving you these painkillers. Take one every few hours for your headache. Do you have any questions?"

"No, thanks a lot, Doc."

"I'll be by to check on you in the morning. Rest up."

He left the room.

Max closed his eyes. *Hmm,* he thought, *that doctor was here for about four minutes, and I'll probably get a bill for twenty bucks! What a racket!*

The door opened, and a nurse walked in. *How is a guy supposed to get any rest when they're in here every five minutes?* he thought.

The nurse had her back to him.

"It's time for your enema, Mr. Chambers!"

"Enema! Why the hell do I need an enema?"

The nurse turned around, and it was Sally, laughing.

"Sally, you little . . . What's with the getup?"

"It's an old Halloween costume. Do I look authentic?"

"You look a lot better than Nurse Hideous. Come here."

He hugged her tightly.

"I was so worried about you, kid. I never would have forgiven myself—"

"Oh, Max, I was worried about you too. Thank you for saving me."

She kissed his cheek. Then she suddenly pulled away.

"Max, you're never going to believe this. I broke the code in the letter!"

"You're right, I don't believe it."

"But I DID! I figured it out from this book!" she said, shoving it toward him.

"*The Girls' Outdoor Cadette Guide.* You mean to tell me the Nazis are using this for their codes?"

"Max, I checked it and double-checked it. It all works out. Look!"

Max looked at the copy they had made of the letter and looked to Sally's notes.

"The code system is on this page," she said, pushing the book into his hands. "It all matches up! Read it!"

Max read the letter:

> *Our presence in New Rochelle has been compromised. Leave as soon as possible. Go to safe house in Elkridge, Maryland. Address is 112 Mountain Road. Wait there for confirmation of drop. Money and papers are under floorboard in front of fireplace. Check post office box 207 for further instructions.*

Max blinked in disbelief. He thought he'd blown the case when the German died, but now it was all right in front of him.

"Sally! Give me a kiss, you little—just give me a kiss!"

He hugged her and kissed her smooth rosy cheek.

"Okay, as soon as the doctor says you can leave, we can hit the road!"

"We're leaving now! Find my clothes! Let's hurry before the Wicked Witch of the West comes back!"

"Here, Carol brought some clothes for you when she heard what happened."

"Okay. Turn around, kid, before you see a side of me that you haven't."

Sally took a long peek at Max's bare buttocks when he stood in his hospital gown. He quickly dressed, and leaning on Sally, they both walked calmly out of the hospital.

"Oh shit, where is my car?"

"Oh no, it's still in front of the post office. Wait here, and I'll go get it."

"I can walk. It's not that far. Just let me lean on you."

They walked the few blocks to the post office with Max's arm around Sally's shoulder. He was too heavy for her, but she said nothing until the car was in sight.

"Max, stop leaning so much. You're too heavy for me."

"Oh, come on, it's right over there."

"You're hurting my back, Max. You're hurting me!"

A man tapped Max on the shoulder.

"Excuse me," he said.

Max turned around and saw a large fist coming toward his face. It was too late to do anything, except feel the full brunt of it on his chin. He toppled head over heels and landed in the street.

Max started to get up to return the favor, but Sally jumped on him.

"It's the man from the post office. He thinks you're my husband," Sally whispered in his ear.

"Don't ever let me hear that you laid a hand on this little lady. Do you hear?"

Max leaned back and nodded.

"Are you all right, Mrs. Wagner?"

Sally nodded.

"You just come see me if he touches you again. Just come see Lew Prest."

With that, Lew Prest marched proudly down the street.

As soon as he was out of earshot, Max and Sally started laughing. Max thought it would have been funnier if he hadn't gotten a bust in the chops, but he still laughed.

"Oh, Sally, the price we pay . . . Remind me never to use the battered-wife plan again."

"Oh, I'll be reminding you—a lot."

# Chapter Twelve

Gino looked at Carol as they were driving. She was silent when not giving one-worded answers to his questions and comments.

"So you really think public speaking is a good career for you?"

Carol just looked at Gino.

"Oh, I'm just fooling around. I know you're worried. Max is gonna be all right."

She smiled at him. Carol liked Gino. He was a gentle soul and always went out of his way to say nice things to her, anything to make her smile. Then her smile faded.

The car pulled up in front of her and Max's house.

"Let me come in and make sure everything is okay."

He had done so the past two days. Even when he came to deliver the bad news about Max, he made sure the doors and windows were all locked.

"Looks like all is well. I'll call you when I'm ready to go to the hospital tomorrow, okay?"

"Th-thank you, Gino. Good night."

"G'night."

Carol closed the door and locked it. She took off her heavy glasses, putting them on the coffee table. She rubbed her eyes and blinked. It wasn't quite dinnertime, so she decided to take her bath. Grabbing a magazine, she headed up the stairs to their bedroom. Kicking off her shoes, she sat on the edge of the bed and removed her slacks. She noticed the hair on her legs. In the bathroom, she took a close look in the mirror at her jet-black hair. Her roots were showing. It was time to color. Looking under the sink, she found the hair dye.

Carol turned the water on in the tub. She stripped. Picking her razor, she began shaving the blond hair from her legs and pubic area.

# Chapter Thirteen

**M**ax drove Sally home. He felt awful about involving her in this business. He tried to think of ways to remove her from the case, but she had been integral so far. He knew he needed a receptionist. That was going to be the reason.

"Listen, kid, umm, I think we'd all be better off with you in the office. I need someone there to handle any calls. This case won't go on forever."

"This case wouldn't be going on at all if it weren't for me! You need me, Max, and you know it!"

"I can't afford to hire another person. Gino is killing me with his 'expenses and fringe benefits.' Another secretary is going to wipe me out!"

"Who do you think has been in the office all these days? My sister, Katherine, has been answering the phone, doing the books, and taking any messages. I go over everything with her at night."

"Katherine? How the hell is she going to handle everything?"

"It's not as if we have a bustling den of activity. The newspapers have been the only calls so far. Plus, she's nineteen, the same age I was when you hired me. She's doing fine."

"How, may I ask, is she getting paid?"

"I'm paying her $5 a day out of my salary."

"But . . . you can't afford that! I can't afford that!"

"She's just an emergency replacement for now. If you like her performance, you can offer her a reasonable salary."

"I don't know whether it's my broken-down condition or you're just too smart for me. All right, we'll keep her there until the case is over. Pay her out of petty cash and take out what you've already paid her. But I'm not making any promises. Let her know that, okay?"

"I already did, Max. You're just so predictable."

He smiled at her reply. She was a great kid to have around the office and proved that she was valuable to have outside the office.

Sally lived in an apartment building on Huguenot Street near Center Avenue. It was a nice place. The Chatter Box, a cute little luncheonette, was on the ground floor. The Connors lived on the fourth floor. They had lived there ever since Sally was born. The rent wasn't too bad, but since her father and elder brother were gone, it was a struggle. Maureen Connors was determined to stay in that apartment for her daughters' sake. She worked as a saleslady at Arnold Constables, a large department store on Main Street. To make ends meet, she took in sewing and usually worked until ten o'clock at night.

"Hi, Mom," Sally said as she walked through the front door.

"You're late. Is everything okay?"

"Oh, it's great! I'm going on a road trip with Max!"

"Oh no, you're not, young lady! A road trip with a married man? Over my dead body!"

"Mom, it's not what you're thinking. His partner is coming along too. I'm actually working on an important case!"

"I thought you were a secretary. Why does he need you to go on a 'road trip'? Are you going to take dictation in his car?"

"Mom, it's investigation. We just have to find someone and interview him."

"Where will you be sleeping, young lady?"

"By myself in a motel room. What do you take me for?"

"Well, I'm going to have to speak with your boss about all this."

"Okay, I'll call him in a little while, and you can talk to your heart's content, but I'm going!" Sally said as she marched to her bedroom and slammed the door.

Sally rolled her eyes and shook her head as she started to get undressed. Hanging up her dress, she caught sight of her framed picture from the office. It was taken when they opened the office, and Max's family threw a party. Max stood with his arm around Sally, and they both had such wide smiles. She was sure that Max was drunk, and she certainly was. She was so proud to be working in the investigative field. *It is almost like being a spy,* she thought. People would come in with their secrets, needing help, and she was part of it. It was just like the movies. And Max was such a good man. He was always nice to her and let her have time off whenever she needed it. Plus, he was so handsome. She had such a crush on him from the moment they met. He treated her like a little sister, but she kept her hopes up that he would notice her in another way.

As she sat on her bed, she realized that she was rocking back and forth with excitement. Escaped Nazis, car chases, this was what she signed up for. Oh, she couldn't wait! After her shower, she would call Max and have him speak to her mother. That ought to satisfy her. Max could be very persuasive. And she had to pack. She stood and jumped up and down. She was so happy.

After dropping Sally off, Max decided to visit Bernstein. Hank must have known about this German who nearly killed him. *Why would he be holding back any information?* Max thought. Something didn't quite jibe about this whole business.

"Good evening, Mr. Chambers! What an honor to have this unexpected visit," said Rabbi Silverman. "We read all about your heroics in the newspaper!"

"How are you, Rabbi? Sorry to drop in like this, but I'd like to talk to Mr. Bernstein. Is he here?"

"Yes, come in."

The rabbi led Max to a large study. Bookshelves rose to the high ceiling all around the room. A large desk sat in a corner, piled with papers. Max took a seat on an overstuffed couch, and Bernstein entered the room.

"Mr. Chambers, Max, how are you? The *Standard Star* wrote all about you. I was starting to get worried."

"So was I, Hank. I was worried when that Nazi abducted my secretary. I was worried when he nearly beat me to death. I was worried when he drove me off a fucking bridge!"

"You expected a Nazi to be gentle?"

"I expected to know who the fuck he was! You gave me a dossier with love letters and Christmas cards, but you couldn't give me a picture of that murdering bastard?! You knew who he was, didn't you?"

"Unfortunately, I did know who he was, but in time, you'll know why I couldn't tell you."

"In time? No, you tell me everything, or I'm through!"

"Oh, now you can't quit after all you've done so far. What would the authorities have to say when they find out about your 'incident' with Karl Schmitt?"

Max leaned back on the couch and lit a cigarette while staring at Hank. He tossed him the pack with a little English on it. It bounced off Hank's chest, and Max held up his Zippo, ready to fling it, but Hank waved him off.

"No, thank you. I have a light."

"You know, I called it when I first met you—blackmail. All that talk about kindness and blankets is giving me the shits!"

"*Blackmail* is an ugly word, Max. There are reasons that I chose you, which you would not understand right now. But there are no more Nazis to worry about, except for Karl Schmitt. Please try to understand. The man you fought with was Hans Brunner. He was a guard at Buchenwald."

Max leaned back and took a deep breath. His head was throbbing like a piston engine, and he ached all over. He needed a good night's rest in his own bed next to his wife. He had no other choice but to trust Hank.

"We decoded a letter to this Brunner character. He was supposed to go to a safe house in Elkridge, Maryland, and wait for the 'drop,' whatever that is. I'm leaving in the morning."

"He is to wait for the 'drop'? Do you know what that means?"

"I was hoping you would know. Is there anything else I need to worry about before I get beaten to death or driven over a bridge?"

"Karl Schmitt will do anything to avoid capture. He knows that he will be executed if captured, so he has, as you say, nothing to lose."

"So you're telling me he's dangerous. Now that's a fucking surprise!"

# Chapter Fourteen

Max breathed a sigh of relief as he pulled into his driveway. He wanted to surprise Carol, so he quietly made his way to the front door and gently turned the key.

"Surprise!"

Carol was lying on the couch, reading a magazine. She jumped when Max came in but quickly ran to him, and they embraced.

"How did you get released so soon? I th-thought you were th-there for a few days."

"I released myself, babe. Hey, where are your glasses?"

"Oh, I could not find them. I have been so w-worried about you."

"Ha, they're on the coffee table, right in front of you, silly."

She quickly put them on and gave Max a deep kiss.

"That's all I needed, honey. The hospital was driving me crazy. Besides, we got a lead on the case. I'm taking a trip in the morning. It'll only be a couple of days. I'll call Julie and Dottie. Maybe they can come over and keep you company."

"Perfect" Julie and "Madame Butterfly" Dottie. They called her "perfect" just to get Mama's goat. Mama thought they were making fun of Julie, but it was just so Mama could get angry and spew forth a slew of Italian and English curse words. She could curse better than a drunken longshoreman. Dottie got her nickname because she was always out with friends or on a date. Max was called Sonny Boy by

Mama, and the girls thought he was spoiled, being the only boy. Papa Chambers usually sat back and enjoyed the entertainment. When things were quiet, he did what he could to get Mama to explode. But Mama really loved the attention deep down.

Max dialed Gino's house and read him the decoded letter. He was also amazed that Sally had broken it and with the book it was from. But he quickly agreed to take the road trip and hung up the phone to get ready.

Max spoke to Maureen Connors and convinced her that everything would be on the up and up. Sally was needed for her dictation skills, and he would be personally responsible for her safety and well-being. He could hear Sally jumping for joy when Maureen gave her okay.

"With me on the job, Max, this case will be solved in no time. I'll see you in the morning!"

Max smiled as he hung up the phone. Sally just had a way about her that was like a breath of fresh air. She was smart, adorable, and single. *What the hell is wrong with the guys in this town that she hasn't been snapped up already?* he thought.

After a light dinner, Max and Carol made their way upstairs. He quickly threw some things into a suitcase and took a long hot shower. He put the radio on and lay down in his soft, warm bed. He stubbed out a cigarette and closed his eyes. Just as he was drifting off, Carol entered the room in a revealing negligee.

"Oh, babe, I don't know if I'm up to it tonight. I'm still recuperating."

"Th-this can only make you feel better. I am all clean, just how you like me."

She pulled back the covers and gave Max a passionate kiss. Her hands easily tore off his pajamas, and she could see that he really was "up to it." Slowly, she pulled down the straps of her negligee and exposed her large firm breasts.

"Oh, you're gonna kill me one of these days, babe."

"Did you miss this in the hospital?" she said as she rubbed her pink nipples in his face.

"Well, there was this one nurse who really made me hot."

"Who?" she asked as she straddled him. "The ugly one who threw us out?"

"She wasn't ugly. She was brutal!" he said with a chuckle. "You, on the other hand, are one hot broad."

Carol removed the rest of her negligee, revealing her clean-shaven vagina. She sat on his erection with a low moan, and they made wild, passionate love.

# Chapter Fifteen

Max slept like a dead man and was woken up by Gino's phone call at 9:00 a.m. After a quick shower and breakfast, he was ready to go.

"Don't worry, Carol, after last night, nothing could keep me away from you."

Carol gave him a deep kiss and rubbed his buttocks.

"Julie is going to give you a call later and come over. Just try to relax, okay?"

"Okay, Max. I love you."

"I love you too, honey."

The familiar strains of "In the Mood" played on the radio as Gino drove south toward Maryland. Max had taken a pain pill and dozed in the passenger seat. From the back seat, Sally complained.

"Oh my god, this sounds like my mother's music! Can't you put something on that was at least recorded in the forties?"

"Hey, this is the kind of music that inspires people," Gino said.

"It inspires people to commit suicide! See if you can find a station that plays Frank Sinatra."

"We're going south. In a little while, all we'll be able to get is country music. I hope you like banjos."

When the song ended, Max turned off the radio.

"All right, as long as we're all going to be here a while, let's put our heads together on this. What the hell is the 'drop'? I'm thinking it's some kind of instructions . . ."

"They were getting instructions from the letters in the post office, so I don't think it's that," Sally said.

"You're right, but why were they using the code from your girl ranger book or whatever it's called? I think there is an American in the middle of this, and that's the only code he could understand. What do you think, Gino?"

"I agree about the American. Some American mixed up with Nazis!"

Sally looked at the signs along Route 1 as they sped through Pennsylvania. They had been driving a few hours, and she was getting hungry.

"Why don't we pull over and get something to eat? I'll be able to think better on a full stomach."

"Gino brought some food, Sally. Check in that brown bag."

Sally pulled out a huge round Italian bread and some dried sausages.

"Gino, what is all this?"

"Man cannot live on bread alone," he said with a laugh.

"It looks like I will be living on bread alone. What am I supposed to do with these things?"

"Toss me one of those things," Max said. "I'll show you how to do this."

He took out his pocketknife and sliced off a hunk of bread. Then he cut a few slices of the sweet Italian sausage and stuffed them in the bread.

"Here, kid, try this. I can't believe you don't know about good Italian food."

"Oh, I loved that stuff your mom brought over at Easter. What was it called, Pizza Putzica?"

"Pizza Rustica! I'm glad she didn't hear you say that."

Pizza Rustica was a special dish only prepared at Easter time. It was basically a big pie filled with ricotta cheese, mozzarella cheese, eggs, ham, and sweet Italian sausage. Max and his sisters usually called it Easter pizza. Mama Chambers would slave over the preparations and make around fifteen to twenty of these huge pizzas. Then she would wait for someone to visit on Easter and give them a pie. If no one called or visited, they didn't get a pizza. Max was convinced that she only made them so that she could hold it over someone's head.

"Mmm, this is good! It's just like salami!" Sally said through a mouthful of sandwich.

"It's better than salami!" Max said as he passed a sandwich to Gino. "Pass me a bottle of soda."

"What is this? Conitto?"

"It's called Chinotto. Take a sip."

"Ooh, tastes like root beer!"

Max rolled his eyes but couldn't help smiling at Sally's culture shock.

"Gino, do you want me to drive a while?"

"With you hopped up on those pills? Hell no! I'd feel safer crashing a plane with Schwimmer!"

Night fell as the car entered Maryland. Using his map, Max was able to guide them to Elkridge and the house at 112 Mountain Road. They cut the headlights as they turned onto the street. It was basically a dirt road with houses about a half mile apart. They stopped the car and walked about fifty yards to the house. It was just a shack. Gino went around the back to see if there was another door and came back quickly when there wasn't.

"Okay, Gino, wait here with Sally. If I'm not back in fifteen minutes, get in the car and find a police station. Don't follow me in."

"Well, why in the hell did you want me to check the house and come back here?"

"I-I-I don't know, Gino. I'm on drugs. What'd you expect? Just don't follow me in unless I give you a heads up."

"I'll take that under advisement, but I don't know if that's what I'll do."

"Nothing happens to the kid! I'm serious!"

"Will you stop it, Max? I'm not a kid, and I can handle myself! You brought me, now trust me!"

"Don't worry, Max, I'll take care of her. Go ahead."

Satisfied, Max slowly made his way to the front door. He had his .45 automatic out, ready for anything. The porch was a creaky collection of wooden planks that sounded like a jazz band in the silence of the night. No lights shone through the windows. Max tried the front doorknob. Locked. Next, he tried one of the front windows, which were unlocked and opened easily. Using his flashlight, he made his way around the place. There was a front room and a back room, and both were empty. He breathed a sigh of relief. Opening the front door, he made his way back to the car, and the three of them drove around the back of the shack and parked so as not to be seen from the road.

"Well, it looks like Hans Brunner was coming to an empty house. It doesn't look like anyone has been here for a while, judging by the dust. What do you think, Gino?"

"There's no food here, and the stove is ice-cold. I think you're right."

Sally checked the fireplace. "This hasn't been used lately."

"There's a bed in that room. We'll stay the night. You and Sally get some rest, and I'll keep watch. I'll wake you in a couple of hours, Gino."

"Oh my god! The bathroom is disgusting! I am not using that!"

"You can use that or the ladies' room outside, kid."

"Very funny! You guys have it easy. You don't have to touch anything in there!"

"All right, let me take a look. Give me a few minutes, and it'll be usable."

"Thank you, Gino. Max, what are you doing?"

"I'm lighting a fire. Hans Brunner was expected here, so we might as well make it look like he's here. The police never identified him, so no one knows that he's dead."

"Uh-huh."

The fire crackled to life and filled the room with a warm breath. Max lit some candles, and the room came to life. There was no electricity, and an old icebox sat empty in a corner.

"You're all set, Sally. The king of England would be proud to take a shit in there now."

"Thank you, Gino. It looks a lot less disgusting now."

"Oh, come on, kid, you're not gonna be taking a bubble bath in there!"

"Max, you just don't understand women."

Max smiled. She was right. He had a hard time understanding women. Take Carol, for example. She read her books and movie star magazines all day but never had anything to say about them. He had to yank every word out of her. She was as quiet as a church mouse around other people but was like a tiger in the bedroom. She dressed like an old librarian during the day but wore the most reveling negligees at night. They had shared every intimate experience that a couple could, yet she wouldn't let Max see her with razor stubble on her legs. They made love almost every night, but she hadn't yet gotten pregnant. It was something that concerned him, but she merely said that it would happen when the time was right. Both Julie and Dottie had children, three each, and Mama always said that she wanted another grandchild. She wanted a Chambers grandchild. Max did too. He wanted to play catch on the lawn with his son. He wanted to take his daughter to piano lessons. He wanted to put a shiny bicycle under the Christmas tree. He wanted all those things and more. He wanted a nice big Italian family of his own. Maybe this was the year that it all came together.

Max literally shook his head to get back in the swing of things. Those pain pills had made him a bit foggy, and it was sheer luck that he hadn't run into trouble here. He took out the thermos and filled a cup with strong coffee. He took a seat by the front window and settled in.

"Holy shit, Max, you forgot about the floorboard, you stupid bastard!"

"Sorry, Gino, I'm still a little out there."

"You got me cleaning the goddamn bathroom!"

Sally came out, and they started looking for a loose plank. They were stomping around like hillbilly clog dancers. Finally, they heard a thud.

"That must be it, Gino!" Max said as he pulled out his pocketknife.

He pried up the board, and there was an old strongbox. It wasn't locked, and he took out a single piece of paper. It was coded the same as the other letter. There was a small envelope containing a key. An American passport was at the bottom.

"Sally, get the book and figure out what this says. This must be for the post office box."

They stood over her shoulders and watched as the letter came to life.

"There it is, boys. Eat your hearts out!"

> *Instructions waiting at Elkridge Post Office. This location has been compromised. Leave immediately for new location. Use passport as your new identity.*

Everyone seemed to sigh in disappointment at the same time.

"Another safe house? They sure are safe from us!"

"I know, kid. If it were so easy, I wouldn't charge $25 a day plus expenses."

"Say, Max, where did you come up with that figure?"

"Gino, I saw it in a Humphrey Bogart movie!"

# Chapter Sixteen

The Elkridge Post Office opened promptly at 9:00 a.m., and the happy crew waited in the car, checking the layout. The street was nearly deserted, and Max thought that it was probably like this every day, including New Year's Eve.

"I'll be going in this time if you don't mind, Sally," Max said. "If any Nazi comes out of the woodwork, I'll shoot him in the balls."

"I don't mind at all. I'm happy to wait here."

"Just try to keep your legs closed and your head out of Gino's crotch."

"Gino, you said you wouldn't tell Max!"

"Sorry. In all the excitement, I almost got head—I mean, I lost my head!" he said, laughing.

Max was laughing aloud as he crossed the street and made his way into the post office. Box 207 was in the middle of a long line of boxes. Max looked in both directions and then toward the car. Gino was giving him a thumbs-up. The coast was clear. He turned the key and removed the single envelope. Max quickly closed the box and made his way toward the car.

"Did you behave while I was gone, kid?"

"I'm not speaking to either of you pigs!"

"Do you think you could speak to us pigs about the code?"

"That I will speak about!"

She quickly slipped the letter out and started decoding. Gino pulled away and drove aimlessly, waiting for the results.

"Okay, I got it!"

It said,

> Go to Red's Roadhouse on Route 41 in Waterford, Virginia. Speak to Red. The code word is DRAGON. Then ask for a glass of white wine.

"Are you sure you got that right?"

"Yeah, kid. Could you double-check that?"

"That's what it says. Do you think I'd make up something like that?"

"Okay, Gino, it looks like we're on our way to Virginia."

"Well, I didn't have anything better to do."

"Wait, we're not far from Baltimore. Let's make a little detour. Maybe I can find Carol's folks."

"I thought you said she did speak to her parents."

"She doesn't. In fact, I can count the number of fights we've had on one hand, and they were all about not wanting anything to do with them. But I think if I could get them together, they would be able to settle things. They are the only family she has."

"Well, family is important. You only get one."

"That's right. I don't know what I'd do without my family around."

"Okay, Baltimore, here we come!"

# Chapter Seventeen

The drive to Baltimore took a little over an hour. They pulled into the first gas station they saw.

"What'll it be, folks?" asked the old attendant.

"Fill it up. Say, do you have any maps inside?"

"Sure do. What are you looking for?"

"I just want one that has the city of Baltimore. Oh, and I need one for Virginia. Do you have those?" Max asked.

"Yep, they're in the office."

"Thanks. I'll be right back, Gino."

Max entered the office and looked for the maps. They were behind the counter. No one seemed to be around, so he rang the bell on the counter. Startled, Max jumped back when a small man immediately stood up behind the counter. He was covered from head to toe in grease, and his head was topped with flaming red hair. He gave Max a wide toothy smile when he paid for the maps. He looked like something out of a minstrel show.

When Max got back to the car, he said, "Hey, Gino, there is a guy back there who looks just like you."

"He must be a handsome chap."

"Oh yeah, Tyrone Power had better watch out."

Max was sure he was doing the right thing. However badly Carol was treated as a child, her folks would have to be happy to see her after all these years.

"Here you are. That'll be $2.75. Are you looking for any place in particular?"

"Yeah, can you tell us how to get to Grand Street?"

"Sure, take this road about a mile and make a left onto Atlantic Street. Follow that about eight or nine blocks, and Grand street will be on your right."

"Thanks a lot, old-timer."

They found Grand Street easily and parked the car. It was a street that looked like it was out of an Andy Hardy movie. Tree lined and cute little houses as far as the eye could see. They stretched their legs and began a leisurely stroll down the street.

"Oh boy, this sure beats my neighborhood," Sally said. "Why would anyone want to leave this?"

"It's what's inside the house that matters, kid. Let us see if we can find number 381."

"How do you know the address?"

"Gino, I looked them up as soon as we were married. I was going to send them a letter, but Carol found out and hit the roof."

"You think she won't hit the roof when she finds them on your doorstep?"

"If they could just see one another, I'm sure things would be different. The last time she saw them was 1943. That's a long time. People change."

Number 381 Grand Street was a beautiful house. It was a white Cape Cod with light blue shutters. A weeping willow tree shaded the front, and manicured bushes lined the walk. Max shook his head when he thought of how terrible things could happen in such an innocent place.

"Okay, let's see how they like their son-in-law," Max said as he rang the doorbell.

A young woman answered the door. "Yes, can I help you?"

"Hi, I'm looking for Mr. or Mrs. Bird."

"There's no one here by that name."

"Andrew and Vera Bird? They don't live here?"

"Afraid not. My husband and I have lived here three years."

"I'm sorry. Did they leave a forwarding address?"

"I've never even heard of them."

"Well, didn't you buy this house from them?"

"If you must know, we bought this house from the bank. It was vacant when we moved in. Now what's this all about?"

"I'm trying to track down my wife's parents, and this was their address. I'm sorry to bother you. Have a good day."

Max slowly walked down the path, shaking his head. Before he could say anything, Gino held up a hand.

"We heard. Tough break, huh?"

"Yup."

"Now what?"

"I don't know. I always had this crazy idea. I never thought they would have moved."

"Hey, city hall was right around the corner. Why don't you try over there? There has to be a record of the sale."

"Yeah, you're right. Let me head over there really quick. You two want to stay here? I'd like to be alone for a bit."

"We'll be here. Take your time."

Sally and Gino watched as Max slowly walked away. He had his head down and looked so disappointed. They sat on the hood of the car, and Sally lit a cigarette. She took a deep drag and let out a sigh of pity.

"I feel so bad for Max. He treats that wife of his like a queen, and all he gets out of her are problems. He does all the shopping. He does all the yard work. He even cleans up after dinner. All she does is lie around the house all day. It's not like she has kids to look after. She just hides in that house."

"Yeah, Sally, you got that right."

"Gino, I get along great with people, but she's just a brick wall."

"What do you mean by that?"

"I mean, she won't talk, not even small talk. I always make a funny comment when I see her, but she never even smiles. Shoot, anyone would smile just to be polite. But not her. I don't know. I just don't like her. You better not say a word of this to Max!"

"Not one word. I won't say a word."

"Ooh look, here comes a mailman. Maybe he knows if there is a forwarding address . . . Excuse me. I was wondering if you could help us."

"I hope so, young lady."

The mailman was an older guy. He was probably about sixty years old and a little stooped from carrying a mailbag for a long time. He had an easy smile, and he put down his bag.

"We're trying to find the people who used to live in that house, number 381. They were named Bird."

"Andrew and Vera Bird. I knew them well and their daughter too. Nicer people you'd never meet."

"Do you know where they moved to?"

"They didn't move. They died. Car crash killed them both about three years ago. It was so sad to see what happened to them. They lost their girl in the war. When she never came back, it just took all the life out of them."

"Can you tell us about them?"

"Oh, they were just the perfect little family, all three of them. He was an accountant. Vera was a teacher. My son went to school with their girl. She was cute as a button, popular too. She was class president, sang in the choir. She played Juliet when they did *Romeo and Juliet* in the glee club. She was going places. But then the war came along, and she joined the WACs. Something happened to her in England, I think. The army said she deserted, but that's a lot of bunk. She never would have left her folks like that. Sad story."

"Thank you very much for your time."

"It's not a problem, little lady. What was it you needed to see them about?"

"Oh, my dad went to school with Mr. Bird. He always told me to look him up if I was in the area. I guess that's not going to happen. But thank you again for your help."

"You're very welcome. You two have a nice day."

They watched in silence as the mailman made his way down the street.

"Gino, that's not Max's wife he was talking about!"

"No, it sure doesn't seem like Carol. Maybe we got the wrong address?"

"The wrong Andrew and Vera Bird with a daughter named Carol, who never came back from the war? I've heard of coincidences, but this is not one of them!"

"Yeah, I think you're right. But I don't know what it means."

"It means she's an impostor! She's probably a Russian spy!"

"A stuttering spy? Even the Russians aren't that stupid. Something must have happened to her in the war. Shell shock or combat fatigue could make a person develop a stammer. A lot of horrible things happened over there, things you couldn't imagine."

"My dad and brother were killed over there, so I know about horrible things."

"Yeah, I'm sorry. I didn't mean to be callous. It must have been terrible for you and your family."

"Oh, that's okay, Gino. But what are we going to tell Max?"

"We're not going to tell Max anything, except that they died, okay?"

"What?"

"If we tell him what the mailman said, it'll drive him crazy. We don't know what happened to Carol over there, and neither does Max. He loves her, and that's all that matters."

"Yeah, you're right. He does love her, although I don't know what he sees in her."

Gino and Sally got back in the car. They were silent for a while, trying to make sense of it all. Soon, Max turned the corner, walking slowly with his head down. He quickly sat in the passenger seat, staring forward.

"Any news?"

"Yeah, Gino, they're dead."

"Yeah, we talked to the mailman. He knew them. I'm sorry."

"I'm sorry too, Max."

"Thanks. I guess we wasted a trip."

"We didn't waste anything. You wanted to do something good for your wife. There's nothing wrong with that. It just didn't work out."

"Yeah, I guess you're right. HEY! What do you say to a trip to the booming metropolis of Waterford, Virginia?"

"I'd say look out, Virginia! Here we come!"

# Chapter Eighteen

"Hi, Julie, how is everything going?"

"Hi, Max. Everything's fine. Where are you?"

"We're on the way to Waterford, Virginia. How's Carol?"

"Oh, she's her usual talkative self."

"Come on now, give her a break."

"Give me a break, big brother. I've had better conversations with the clothesline."

"Are you saying this where she can hear you?"

"No, she's not here. She wanted to go for a walk. It's just me and the kids."

"I really appreciate you hanging out with her."

"Don't be silly, Max. That's what family does."

"Okay, let me get off this phone. Tell Carol I called, and I'll try back later on, okay?"

"Oh wait! Nick Kemp was here yesterday. He said that the funeral for Jimmy is on Saturday."

"Oh shit, I didn't think it'd be so soon. I'll think of something. Take it easy, Julie."

"I will, and you be careful. Bye-bye."

"Bye."

Max trotted back to the car and quickly got in. Gino was checking the map and planning the route. Sally was nervously chewing a nail in the back seat.

"Is everything okay?"

"Yeah, Sally, everything's fine. Julie was there with the kids. Carol was out for a walk. Nicky Kemp came by and said Jimmy's funeral is set for Saturday."

"Well, it's only Tuesday. We can make it back by then. What do you think, Gino?"

"I guess it depends on what we find in Virginia."

"Well, what are we waiting for? Do you think you can drive this crate any faster than you've been?"

"Max, you ain't seen nothing yet. Hold on to your balls!"

"Speak for yourself. Remember that I'm a lady."

"Sorry, I forgot the back seat."

Gino quickly drove out of town and headed west. It was a long way to Virginia, and everyone was quiet for a while. Max was deep in thought. He didn't know what he was going to say at the funeral. He rubbed his face and felt his heavy stubble. He needed a shave. Maybe they would stay in a motel tonight, and he could shower and shave. He looked over at Gino.

"Hey, Gino, what is that on your lip?"

"Oh this? It's my mustache. How's it looking?"

"It looks like you just drank Ovaltine!" Max said with a laugh.

"Hey, it works for Errol Flynn!"

"Gino, you're about as far from Errol Flynn as Red Skelton!"

"Yeah, you say that now. Remember that movie he made about Burma? That was based on my exploits in the war."

"You never set one foot in Burma."

"Hey, my planes took enough Jap flak from Burma that they should have made me an honorary citizen!"

"Okay, I'm too tired to argue about it."

"You know, that reminds me about Jimmy. You know we never got along."

"I know, Gino. I know you put up with him because we were friends, and I appreciate it."

"No, that's not what I was getting at. He was always such a nasty guy. When I was in the first grade over at Columbus School, this kid was beating me up. I was the only Italian with red hair, so I stood out. I'll always remember that the kids around were egging him on, and Jimmy was one of them."

"Yeah, but that was ages ago."

"I know, but he was always picking on someone. All the time we were growing up, he seemed to need to act superior to someone. What really got under my skin was something that happened right before we went in the service. We all went to see that Errol Flynn movie where he was General Custer. The bad guy in the movie was talking about gold. Gold would make people sit up and take notice of you. Gold and glory, something that no one could take away from you. Jimmy kept repeating that when we left."

"It's just a movie, Gino. I remember that night. It was probably the last time we were all together."

"I'm not finished. We all piled into my car and were driving down Main Street when Jimmy spotted that Scobie kid, Allen Scobie. He said, 'There's that fag Scobie. Pull over, Gino.' I said, 'What for?' He said, 'So we can beat his ass. He's a fag!' I said, 'What's it to you? Leave the guy alone. He's not hurting anyone.' Then Jimmy started calling me a fag lover and stupid stuff like that. I just thought that this guy had something seriously wrong with him."

"I remember that too. I thought you showed a lot of class, so did the girls."

"Yeah, it scored some points, but that's not why I did it. It was wrong."

"Jimmy really changed over the years. He was always nicer to me than he was to you, Gino. The war really changed him. He was like a different person over there. He was always looking for something that would make him hero. He wanted a chest full of medals so when he went home, he could write his own ticket. I heard him say that a million times. I guess he really was looking for gold and glory. In the end, he didn't get either of them."

Sally leaned her arms across the front seat and rested her head.

"Max, what was it like over there?"

"Oh, there was a lot of shooting and praying."

"No, I mean at that camp where they killed all those people, Buchenwald."

"Don't ask him about that stuff. It's not something he wants to talk about. It'll be too much for you."

"I lost my dad at Anzio. My brother was killed in Okinawa. That's not too much for me."

"That's okay, Gino. You really want to know, kid?"

"Yes, Max, please."

"It was a huge place. I went in at one of the sub-camps. It wasn't very big. There were maybe about ten buildings. One was filled with about a thousand poor guys, but it was made to hold about fifty horses. Most of the Nazis had deserted by the time we got there, but we had to fight our way in. When we got to the main camp, there was a big metal gate with the words 'Arbeit Mach Frei' over the top. That means work makes you free. I can't describe the smell that wafted over that place. I don't think anyone can. They had a whole shitload of buildings filled with people. They were people who were down to their last hours. They were skeletons. I didn't think anyone could ever be that emaciated and still alive. They were tattooed with numbers on their arms. Women and children too. There were buildings filled to the roof with eyeglasses, shoes, empty suitcases. Another was filled with hair, women's hair, which was made into cloth. They said it was for the U-boat crews. They also made pillows from the hair. Another building contained all the valuables taken from the people as they arrived. It had art, money from all over Europe, musical instruments, picture frames, and gold. I saw a huge barrel filled with gold teeth.

"They had a gas chamber that looked like a shower. It even had fake showerheads on the ceiling. Most of the women and children and old people were gassed as soon as they arrived. When the others were too weak to work, they were gassed too. They were given soap and told to breathe deeply, and the shower would help them. The lucky ones never suspected what was going to happen until it was too late. Then they locked the doors, and a crew on the roof dropped rat poison into the vents. It was called Zyklon B. I think it was cyanide. Every poor soul in that chamber would be dead in about fifteen minutes."

Max spoke in a quiet, even tone. His voice cracked from time to time, but he continued as if he was a robot. Tears poured from his eyes, but he went on. Sally was crying, and Gino was slowly shaking his head in disbelief.

"Then there was a crew who took out the dead bodies and cut them open. The Nazis wanted to be sure that no one had swallowed or inserted anything of value like a wedding ring or grandma's ruby broach. They picked fellow prisoners to do this. They gave them extra food or something.

"There was a crematorium. It was made by a company that made baking ovens. They were so proud of it that they had a plaque inscribed with the company name mounted on it. Here was where they burned the bodies. They were given orders to kill and cremate every last inmate before we arrived. There were too many people for them to carry out the order, but they tried. They burned some of the people alive. The rest of the bodies were stacked like cordwood in a couple of other buildings. The faces of the dead showed the horror that they'd been through.

"The next day Ike showed up, so did Bradley and Patton. We were told to bring the townspeople up to the camp and show them every last detail of what went on. They set up a table with some of the trophies of the Nazis. There was a lampshade made from skin, a couple of shrunken heads, and evidence that they tried to make soap out of the Jewish bodies. I guess you need fat to make soap, but the poor people were so starved that that experiment failed.

"Edward R. Murrow was there. He did a report, but he couldn't tell the whole story. It was too much for people to hear. A lot of guys got sick to their stomachs, Patton too. Old Blood and Guts spilled his guts. All the townspeople were horrified. They never had any idea of what was going on, not a clue. The ungodly smell permeated through their village, but they never knew what was happening. Trainloads of people went through the town, but no one ever asked where they were going and why the trains left empty.

"You know, the toughest thing was that we weren't allowed to feed these people! We all went to the town and took every last bit of food from every store and bakery and butcher shop to feed them, and we were told to stop. They said you can't feed people who have forgotten how to eat. We had to take it all away! The medics made a special soup for them to eat. I can't tell you how many died after we got there, hundreds, maybe a thousand.

"A couple of soldiers cracked up. Either they cried uncontrollably or they went catatonic. They took twenty or thirty guys to the army hospital. I don't know what happened to them. I guess they got better, who knows. Some guys took it out on the Nazis who were captured. They were either shot or given to the mobs of inmates. I'm guilty of that. I threw one guy into the mob, and they tore him apart. Our friend Bernstein was there, and he remembered me. That's what he's holding over my head, and that's why we're driving to fucking Virginia when I should be home with my wife.

"So, Sally, do you have an idea of what it was like?"

"I'm so sorry, Max, you poor thing," she said, giving him a tearful hug.

"It gets better. I ordered Jimmy Kemp and another guy named Frazier to take the rest of the guards back to headquarters. Jimmy wanted to stay and get in on the credit, but his truck hit a land mine, and everyone was killed, burned to cinders, everyone except Karl Schmitt, this Hans Brunner character, and some other guy. Schmitt switched uniforms with a private, the same private whom I threw to the crowd. That is how Jimmy died.

"Fucking Nazis. How could they even dream up something so depraved? If you gave me a hundred years, I could never come up with something that evil. And they all went along with it too! No questions asked. Why should they? They were getting the homes of their neighbors who were dragged away at any time of the day or night. Of course, no one was ever a member of the Nazi party. You couldn't find a Nazi in Germany. You couldn't even find any one who ever voted for Hitler. That cute little town that we went into was filled with those kinds of Germans. They never knew what was going on in the camp. But everywhere you went in that fucking town you could smell that ungodly stench. They were shocked, when we brought them up there. We made them bury all the bodies and clean up the place.

You know, even if one of those people were telling the truth, what did they think was happening when the Jews were taken away? What did they think when they gleefully reported a Jew hiding in an attic? What were they thinking when the Jews were murdered in the streets in broad daylight? What can you do with people like that?"

"Don't worry, Max, we'll get him. One down one to go."

"I hope so, Gino."

# Chapter Nineteen

"You know, Julie, we came to spend time with Mrs. Talkative, and she goes out! What gives?" Dottie said, shaking her head.

"I don't know, but Max is going to have to babysit a bunch to pay us back," Julie said.

Julie and Dottie were lounging in Max's living room, listening to the radio. They had both married young, right out of high school, to Italian boys, to Mama and Papa's relief. Julie and Eddie lived "up the west" on Fifth Street. That was the Italian section of New Rochelle. Eddie was a good guy who seemed to know everyone in town. He owned a taxi and made a decent living. They had two girls, Robyn, aged nine, and Holly, aged seven, and a son, Anthony, who was three. Julie said the "shop was closed"; three children were enough.

Dottie and Gus had three boys—Michael, aged seven, and Stephen, aged six. Her youngest, Peter, was barely a year old and was sleeping in his carriage parked in the kitchen. Gus had his own auto body shop and also made a good living. They lived on Charles Street, not quite "up the west" but right on the fringes. Michael and Stephen were real hellions. Not a week went by without a broken window or a trip to the emergency room with various injuries.

The cousins all played well together. They rarely fought. The boys liked to climb trees and play ball. The girls were typical girls. They liked their baby dolls and toy strollers. Little Anthony was anything but little. He was huge for his age. Mama Chambers loved to babysit and basically fed him a meatball every time he cried. When Max was around, he would snatch the meatball from the boy, enraging Mama.

Max really liked to babysit. He would have kids spend the night, and they would camp out in the living room. They all loved it when Max told them ghost stories and made-up funny stories about Mama and Papa Chambers. During the summer, Max would get them up at the crack of dawn, and they'd go to the beach, either Glen Island or Hudson Park.

"She's been gone for nearly two hours! I thought she said she was going for a short walk," Dottie said.

"Yup, that's what she said. I don't know how much longer I can stay. I have to get dinner ready. Where the hell did she go?"

"Here she comes now."

"It's about time."

Carol entered breathlessly. "I'm sorry. I lost track of the time. I'm so w-worried about Max."

"Oh, that's all right," Julie said. "The kids have been having a great time, and we got to relax. Where did you go?"

"Oh, just around th-the neighborhood. Let me get out of these shoes. My feet are hurting me," Carol said as she walked upstairs.

Julie and Dottie looked quizzically at each other.

"Around the neighborhood? For two hours? I think that's a lot of bull!" Dottie whispered.

"Yeah, me too. She better not be stepping out on Max."

"Shush, here she comes."

Carol poured herself a cup of coffee and joined the sisters. She closed her eyes and put a hand to her head.

"Oh, I have such a headache."

"Why don't you lie down and take a nap? We've got to take off now anyway," Julie said.

"I think I will."

"Oh, Max called while you were out. He said everything is okay. They're on their way to Virginia."

"Good."

"What's so good about that?"

"Nothing. I, uh, uh, meant th-that it is good that everything is okay."

"Oh okay. I let him know about the funeral on Saturday."

"What?"

"I said I let him know about Jimmy Kemp's funeral on Saturday."

"Why did you do that?"

"What's wrong?"

"I, uh, uh, didn't want him to get upset! I w-was hoping that he w-would miss it. He gets so upset when he talks about Jimmy."

"Well, he's supposed to give the eulogy. I think he'd be more upset if he missed the funeral. Maybe this will give him some closure. I'm sorry. I didn't think you would have a problem with that."

"Th-that's all right. I just w-worry about him so much."

"It'll be fine, you'll see."

"I hope so."

They quickly packed up the children and were gone in minutes. Carol watched from the porch as they drove off and waved goodbye. She made her way inside and locked the door. She took off her glasses, picked up the phone, and dialed.

"Long distance, please."

# Chapter Twenty

The drive to Waterford, Virginia, was taking longer than they thought. It had started raining as soon as they left Baltimore, and when night fell, visibility was poor. The Blue Moon Motel was the first one they spotted when it was decided to stop for the night. One room was all that was available. It had two full-size beds.

"All right, I'll take this bed. Sally, you and Gino can sleep together."

"Ha ha, very funny."

"Hey, what's so funny about sleeping with me?" Gino said with mock surprise.

"You two are pigs. I hope you know that. I'm getting in the shower first. Meanwhile, maybe someone could pick up something to eat. Hamburgers would be nice, hint, hint."

"Yes, ma'am. Come on, Gino, let's see what we can find."

There was a greasy spoon right next door to the motel, and they picked up burgers, french fries, and a few bottles of Coke. When they got back to the room, Sally was just out of the shower. She was in pajamas and a robe with her head wrapped in a towel.

"Holy shit, it's an Arab!" Gino shouted with a laugh.

"I'm a hungry Arab, so let's eat!"

They ravenously devoured their dinner, after which Max and Gino took turns showering and getting ready for bed. Sally got into her bed.

"I can only imagine what my mother would say if she knew I was sleeping in a motel room with two men."

"I think I can," Max said. "She'd say you were a floozy, a tramp, and a slut."

"Thanks for clearing that up."

"Hey, some of my best girlfriends were floozies, tramps, and sluts," Gino said.

They all had a good laugh. They were giddy from being so tired. Gino told a dirty joke he'd heard as a child, and they roared with laughter. Then Sally and Max took turns with old jokes, and they were soon in tears, laughing till their sides ached.

"Listen, kid," Max said, giggling, "you can say the first time you were in a motel, it was with two guys, and everyone had a ball!"

The cackling died down, and Max climbed into bed next to Gino. He turned out the light and stared up at the ceiling. Sally had fallen asleep almost immediately; he noticed by her breathing.

"Hey, Gino?"

"Yeah?"

"Do you think we're doing the right thing? I've got a funny feeling about all this."

"We're following up on the only clues we have. Why does that seem funny to you?"

"It's just a feeling in my gut. I don't know, maybe I'm too tired."

"I guess we'll find out when we get to Virginia."

# Chapter Twenty-One

Sally awoke at six thirty the next morning. The room was pitch-black since the curtains were drawn, and she made her way to the bathroom. She was glad that the men were still asleep. She didn't want them to see her before she had time to fix her face and brush her short blond hair. After putting on her lipstick, she went back to the room and turned on the lights. She laughed aloud when she saw how the guys were sleeping. Max was on his side, and Gino was spooning him with his arm around Max's waist.

"Good morning, you lovebirds! I wish I had a camera!"

Max opened his eyes and realized that he was being hugged from behind. He jumped immediately out of the bed.

"Gino, what the hell?!"

"It's a good thing you woke up," he said, rubbing his eyes. "I was dreaming that you were Rita Hayworth."

"Now I've got dirt on both of you. So anymore wisecracks and I'll spill the beans!"

They were dressed and out of the motel in no time at all. Coffee and buttered rolls were breakfast, which they ate in the car. Gino was doing the driving as usual, and Max was checking the map. It was going to be a few hours before they got to Waterford. Max was unusually quiet.

"Are you okay, Max?" Sally said from the back seat. "You haven't said a word all morning."

"Oh, I'm fine, kid. I was just thinking about what I'm going to say at the funeral."

"Well, I don't think they should have imposed on you. You have enough to worry about without having to make up a glowing tribute to that guy."

"It's not like I never think about him. It's always somewhere in my mind. I am glad that they're bringing him home."

In 1947, the United States began the monumental task of identifying and reinterring their war casualties. Both in Europe and the Asia-Pacific, the dead were buried in military cemeteries. If the families chose, the bodies were shipped home to be interred in local cemeteries or the family plots. The dead from Europe were loaded onto ships, which ultimately landed in a large makeshift warehouse in Brooklyn. With the utmost care and respect, the remains were prepared for reinterment. From Brooklyn, the caskets were shipped by rail to their final resting places. They were marked "Do Not Open"; embalming was a luxury that war did not permit.

It was early afternoon when the car pulled up to Red's Roadhouse. It didn't look like anything special, more like a general store. Three cars were parked in the lot, which was just a dirt patch. Max checked his .45 automatic, and Gino followed suit.

"All right, we're going to play this nice and easy," Max said as he lit a cigarette. "Everybody, follow my lead and stay alert. Sally, you stay by my side."

"Okay, Bogie," she said, getting out of the car.

"One more word out of you and I'll plug you, sweetheart," he said, imitating Humphrey Bogart.

He had to smile at the wisecrack. She was really showing her mettle, and he liked what he saw. Gino stretched his legs and pulled his hat down, nearly covering his eyes.

Red's Roadhouse looked like an Old West saloon. In the dim light, Max could see that the long bar took up one side of the room. Nine or ten round wooden tables dotted the rest of the bar. All it needed was swinging doors, and Gary Cooper would have been at home in one of his movies. They sidled up to the bar, and each took a seat on the rough wooden stools.

"What'll it be, folks?" asked the amiable bartender.

"I'm looking for Red," Max said.

"You're looking at him. What can I do for you?"

Red was a chubby little guy wearing a red flannel shirt and a dingy white apron. Max thought he must have had red hair at one point, but what little he had was all gray as was his scruffy beard.

"Dragon," Max said, "and a glass of white wine."

Red eyed him suspiciously, and Max stared back at him. He went to the cash register and took out an envelope and brought it back to Max.

"Care for something to drink?"

"Sure, scotch rocks."

"Make it two," Gino added.

"Three," Sally said, to the amusement of her partners.

"On the house," Red said with a smile.

Max left a dollar tip, and they made their way to the farthest table. Sally took out her girl ranger handbook and watched as Max opened the envelope.

"It's not coded this time," Max said in a low voice.

He spread it out on the table for all to see.

> *Go to safe house in Milwaukee, Wisconsin. Address is 1438 Acorn Drive. We'll be waiting there. Everything is ready.*

No one said anything for a minute. The message was clear, but Max was slowly shaking his head.

"Is it just me, or does anyone think we're being sent on a wild-goose chase?"

"I was thinking the same thing," Gino added.

"I don't understand," Sally said. "What purpose would it serve to have us driving all over the country?"

"It would take us away from where they really are. We found that Brunner character in New Rochelle, and ever since then, we've been out here in the sticks!" Max said, standing. "I've got to hit the head."

No sooner did the bathroom door close behind Max than the front door swung open, and two burly men burst into the bar. They went directly to the bar, and Red put a bottle of beer in front of each of them.

"Well, if it ain't a couple of guinea wops from New York. Jesus, Red, you let these grease balls drink in here?" said the first man.

"Shit, I can smell 'em from here. They almost smell like niggers," the other man added.

They were both wearing filthy overalls and baseball caps. Mud-covered work boots covered their feet, and long unkempt beards rounded out their faces.

Gino looked at them with a wry smile and kicked Sally under the table.

"So you don't like guineas?" he asked.

"No! Why don't you all go back and hang out with Mussolini?"

"Okay, let me see if I got this straight. You don't like guineas, and you don't like niggers. Anyone else?" Gino asked with mock interest. "How about Jews or Polacks?"

"I ain't got any use for you, nigger lovers, or your Jew boys!"

"Oh jeez, I'm going to have to write this down," he said, pulling out a small pad and pencil. "Now let's see, you don't like guineas, Jews, Polacks, and niggers. Am I right so far?"

They walked over to the table and leaned over on each side of Gino and Sally.

"Oh wait, what about Joe DiMaggio?"

"He's a damn Yankee wop!" said the second man through a toothless smile.

"Oh brother, this list is getting longer by the minute."

"Hey, little lady," this first man said loudly, "hows about we take you out back and fuck you like a dirty whore?"

"Is that your best pick-up line?" Sally asked, looking at him with a bored expression.

He opened his mouth to reply, but only a grunt came out. Max had walked up behind him and planted a vicious kick to his balls. As he bent over in agony, Max grabbed a handful of greasy hair and slammed his head into the rough wooden table. Gino immediately cracked the beer bottle across his buddy's face and watched as he hit the floor with a loud thud.

"Listen, you shitkicker! Maybe that's the way you talk when you fuck your sister, but you don't say that shit to a lady!" Max hissed in the ear of his groaning hick. "Now why don't you lie down like a nice hillbilly?" he said, shoving him to the floor.

"Don't do anything stupid, Red!" Max yelled as he saw the bartender moving to the other end of the bar. "Keep your hands where I can see them!" Red froze in his tracks. "Let's get out of this shit hole."

"Nobody says that about Joe DiMaggio around me!" Gino said to his fallen victim.

They made their way to the door, stepping over the guy whom Gino had knocked down. Once outside, Max quickly shoved Sally into the car. The two men came staggering outside, yelling threats.

"Don't let us catch you here at night! We'll be with our Klan brothers! You won't know us, but we'll know you!" yelled the first man, waving an ax handle at Gino.

"I'll know you. You'll be the one with shit stains on his sheet!" Gino yelled back.

He advanced on Gino with the club held high. Max drew his pistol and, with one shot, blew it out of the hand of the bleeding man.

"Get back inside, hillbilly!" Max yelled. "I won't mind putting the next one between your eyes!"

That stopped him in his tracks, and he watched as the car peeled out of the lot, leaving a great cloud of dust.

"Where are we going next, Max?"

"Home, James. Enough of this shit! We're going home, Gino."

# Chapter Twenty-Two

Gino drove as fast as the speed limit allowed, while Max checked nervously over his shoulder. He noticed Sally sitting wide-eyed and silent in the back seat.

"You did well back there, kid," Max said. "You can relax now. Those hicks won't be following us. It's the sheriff I'm worried about. They're all related somehow down here."

"It's not them. I just never saw you shoot a gun before. It was so loud, and you hit that club with one shot!"

Max chuckled with pride. He became a pretty good shot in the war, but even he was surprised that he hit the club with his first shot. The car passed the county line, and he relaxed.

"All right, class, what did we learn today?"

"We learned that they don't like guineas down here!" Gino said with a laugh.

"That's right. Only how did they know we're Italians? We weren't waving the Italian flag and carrying pictures of Mussolini."

*Mussolini, now there was a real asshole,* Max thought. Italian-American relations were set back a hundred years because II Duce partnered up with Hitler. He didn't know how many Americans were killed by the Italians, but every one of them was a slap at people like Max's folks. They'd left Italy long before Mussolini took over, but that didn't make any difference. It was the same with German Americans, maybe even worse. But no one had it worse than Japanese Americans. They were sent off to camps in the desert and lost all their possessions.

"That's right, Max. They were waiting for us. But how would those two jerks know about that Nazi we're looking for?" Sally asked.

"Well, the message wasn't coded this time. There wasn't any key to a PO box. The whole thing seemed sloppy like it was rushed or something."

"Well, whoever wanted us out of town succeeded," Gino added.

"Yeah, that they did. Some private eye I turned out to be."

"Don't blame yourself. There are three of us in this."

"That's right, Gino. We did about as well as the Marx Brothers!"

They traveled north on Route 11 till night fell and pulled off in Martinsburg. It was a bigger city that they expected and found a nice-looking motel. Max didn't feel like eating burgers again, so after checking in, they went looking for a restaurant. The Main Street Steakhouse looked like a decent place. *It is crowded for a Wednesday night, so the food must be good,* Max thought.

The maître d' placed them in a corner booth and took drink orders; scotch on the rocks for everyone.

"All right, Sally, I can't ignore this any longer. How is it that you drink straight scotch?" Max asked.

"I'm Irish! We drink scotch like you Italians drink wine, silly. My dad gave me my first taste when I was twelve years old. I thought he was drinking ginger ale and took a big gulp. I saw him watching me, waiting for me to choke, so I swallowed it and pretended it was nothing. It tasted like gasoline! But I got used to it, and now that's all I drink. Like I drink all the time!"

A good laugh was had all around, and they toasted.

"Here's to the Marx Brothers' detective agency!" Max said, raising his glass.

"I'll drink to that," Gino added.

"There is a lady here, remember? Do you know those 'road' movies with Bob Hope, Bing Crosby, and Dorothy Lamour? We should call it The Road to New Rochelle Detective Agency."

"You got it, Sally! I'll definitely drink to that!" Max said, laughing.

Dinner was delicious. They all had thick steaks with all the trimmings. Gino kept sending his back until it looked like a piece of charcoal, but that was how he wanted it. Dessert was hot apple pie and coffee. The whole dinner cost only $6.75. Max left a nice tip, and they had a leisurely walk back to the motel.

"Jesus, if I lived down here, I'd eat like a king," Gino said, rubbing his full belly.

"You'd go broke having to buy bigger pants!" Max said with a chuckle.

"Max, why couldn't we get two rooms? I'd like a little privacy."

"Sally, you are going to be by my side until we settle this case."

"It looks like I'll be by your side for a long time."

"Thanks very much for the vote of confidence."

The room had two twin beds, and Max had them bring in a folding bed.

"Gino, after last night, I'll feel safer sleeping alone."

"No one wants to sleep with me, the story of my life."

"Don't worry, Gino, one day you'll find someone. Just look at me and Carol. I couldn't have been luckier."

"Yeah, you got lucky, all right."

"Yeah, Max, lucky," Sally said. "I'm getting the shower first."

Everyone took their turns in showering and settled into their beds. No one said anything for a while until Max broke the ice.

"I don't think I'm saying anything groundbreaking, but I think the trail has officially gone ice-cold. Does anyone disagree?"

"Well, you know how I hate to agree with you," Gino said, "but I think you're right."

"What about Mr. Bernstein? You said you thought he was holding back something."

"Listen, kid, all he did was nearly get us killed and have us driving out in the middle of nowhere."

"Max, stop calling me kid!"

"I'm sorry, ms. Connors. I don't trust Bernstein. I don't know what game he's playing, but I don't think it's on the level."

Max leaned back on his bed with one arm behind his head and slowly pulled on a cigarette. Sally was on her stomach, her arms folded under her chin, and she stared at Max. She looked at his handsome face, his perfect profile, his strong chin, and his full lips. *God, how I love him,* she thought. Not in the brotherly/sisterly way he thought of her but in the most romantic way. He was her idea of the perfect man. He was strong yet sensitive. He was self-assured but not afraid to admit defeat. He was her hero even before he had saved her from that brutal Nazi and before he defended her honor from that nasty hillbilly. He was also being taken advantage of by his wife, whoever she was.

Gino cleared his throat, and Sally looked over at him. She realized that he had been watching her the whole time, and she blushed. Gino slowly shook his head from side to side. She knew what he meant. Max was in love with his wife, and Sally wasn't going to change that. It would have to be his decision if and when he found out the truth about Carol Bird Chambers.

# Chapter Twenty-Three

The drive back to New Rochelle was depressing. Max felt as if he'd been had. The closest he was ever going to get to Karl Schmitt was when he was being beaten to death by Hans Brunner. He shook his head, thinking about how gullible he'd been. The notes and PO boxes had all been engineered to keep him out of New Rochelle, while Karl Schmitt presumably escaped. But why was he there in the first place?

Sally dozed in the back seat, while Gino did his best to cheer up Max. He brought up how the two rednecks had tried to rough them up. He showed him the list he started making of all the different ethnic slurs that they heard.

"You know, the sad part is that they think we are the crazy ones."

"Yeah, I know, Gino," Max said, shaking his head. "Let's see, they don't like niggers, Jews, guineas, Polacks, and wops. They were too stupid to know that wops and guineas are the same thing. Assholes."

Gino was quiet. Max saw that he had a quizzical look on his face.

"What's the matter? You don't think that they were assholes?"

"No, it's not that. Something stinks."

"What stinks?"

"Who did you tell that we were going to Elkridge?"

"I told Carol."

"You told her, and then you called me on the phone."

"Yes."

"Who did you tell that we were going to Virginia?"

"I told Carol. No, I told Julie, and I told her to tell Carol."

"Okay."

"Okay what? We're playing twenty questions, and you don't give me the answer. What's on your mind?"

"The way I see it is either Julie or Carol is behind all this or your telephone has been tapped."

"Holy shit! Well . . . I don't think my wife or my sister would want us killed. Maybe my sister would," he said with a laugh.

"If you were married longer, I would bet on your wife wanting you dead!" he said as they both laughed. "But it all adds up. You called me and say that we're going to Maryland. We get to Elkridge, and the message tells us to go to Virginia. You called home and told them our plans. When we get to Red's Roadhouse, there's a welcome party waiting for us."

"Yeah, calling us New York guineas was the giveaway."

"Uh-huh."

"And another thing," Max said, raising his right hand and pointing his index finger, "did you happen to notice on our way out of there a pickup truck on the side of the road? They were working on a flat tire, and they were pointing at us as we passed. I think they were supposed to be the rest of our welcome party."

"Yeah, now that you mention it, but I didn't think much of it at the time."

"OOHHH!" shouted Sally from the back seat, startling Max and Gino.

"What happened, kid? Did a spring pop out of your seat?"

"Don't be silly, Max. They must have wanted to keep us out of the way. Something is going to happen in New Rochelle!"

"I think you are right, Sally. Gino, pull over at the next place that has a phone."

"What are you going to do?"

"If someone is listening, let's let them hear our plans. If they think we are going to Wisconsin, we might be able to catch them off guard."

"Yeah," Gino said, "but who is THEM, and where do we catch THEM off guard?"

"Maybe our friend Bernstein will have another surprise in store for us. I would love to give him a surprise for once."

"That sounds like a plan."


"Hey, babes, how are you?"

"Oh, Max, it's so good-d to hear your v-voice? I m-miss you so much!"

"I miss you too, honey. How's everything going?"

"Everything is fine. Where are you?"

"We are in Virginia."

"Did you get everything done that you needed? I w-want you to come home."

"We got what we needed to get, but I'm not on my way home."

"Where are y-you going?"

"We have to go to Wisconsin, which is a couple of days from here."

"Oh my g-goodness, b-but you have the funeral on Saturday."

"I know, but this is important. You know I can't tell what I'm doing, but I think we're almost finished with this case."

"I cannot w-wait."

"Don't worry, this will be over very soon."

"I love you, Max."

"I love you too, baby. Listen, I really have to get going now. I'll call you tomorrow."

"Okay, Max, goodbye.

"Bye."


Carol hung up the telephone and breathed a sigh of relief. Moving to the record player, she put the needle back on her record, Beethoven's Ninth Symphony. She loved the classics and opera. She never could "get" the popular music of the day; it just had no structure or depth.

The "masters," she thought, *would be rolling in their graves if they could hear what passes for music these days.*

Humming along to the music, she made her way to the kitchen for dinner. Leftover beef stew and a glass of beer was her dinner. She ate quickly and washed the dishes. On her way upstairs to bathe, the doorbell rang. *It is probably Julie or Dottie coming back for something they had forgotten,* she thought. She put on her glasses, which were on the stand by the door. She opened the door, and her mouth fell open.

"Good evening, *fräulein*," said Heinrich Bernstein.

# Chapter Twenty-Four

It was a little after 6:00 p.m. when Max and the crew pulled into Pittsburgh. They decided to stop there for the night, and they would probably arrive back in New Rochelle the next afternoon. After checking in to the Sleep Easy Motel and freshening up, they went out in search of a nice place for dinner but not before Max had a rollaway bed brought to the room. He wasn't taking any chances sleeping with Gino.

Not more than a few blocks from the motel, there was a fancy-looking place called Mario's. In addition to the tables, they were pleasantly surprised that there was a band and a dance floor. Max noticed that Sally had changed into another nice dress that showed off her figure. *Boy,* Max thought, *she really will be a prize for some lucky guy one day—blond hair, blue eyes, long legs, and a nice figure.*

The waiter was named Gino, and they all had a laugh over that while sipping their first round of scotches. Sally quickly finished hers and was on her third drink when the dinner was served, steaks all around. Of course, Gino sent his back until it was burned to a crisp.

"How can you eat that, buddy?" Max asked. "It looks like a piece of charcoal."

"I can't eat raw meat. Take a look at yours. It's still breathing!"

"It is medium rare, buddy. They say it feeds your blood."

Sally went to the ladies' room after they were finished, and on her way back, she stopped to talk to the bandleader.

"Are any of you gentlemen going to ask a lady to dance?" she asked with her hand on Gino's shoulder.

As he started to rise, she pushed him back into his seat. Max had been staring out the window and was surprised by the silence.

"Me? I don't know, kid. This sounds like a jitterbug. I can't cut a rug anymore."

She continued looking at him.

"Okay, okay, I'll give it a whirl but don't expect Fred Astaire," he said as he took her hand, and they made their way to the dance floor.

Gino shook his head as he watched them walk off.

Sally nodded to the bandleader, and the lively music stopped. They immediately started playing a slow love song. Max was relieved at the change of music.

"This is more my style," he said as he took Sally in his arms and waltzed to the tune.

She melted in his arms and placed her head on his shoulder, holding him tight. It had been a long time since Max had danced. In fact, it was his wedding night when he last danced with Carol. They were mustered home days later and hadn't been out dancing since.

Sally felt as if she'd died and gone to heaven. She was in the arms of her hero, and the music, helped by the scotch, made her feel as if she was floating across the dance floor.

Max had closed his eyes, lost in thoughts about Carol, and suddenly realized that he was getting aroused by this woman in his arms. Sally was rubbing her firm breasts against his chest and had her hips planted against his. He loosened his grip and actually blushed when she looked in his eyes. Her eyes were saying what she wished he would say, and she tightened her hold on him. Their faces were inched apart when she opened her mouth slightly, waiting for a kiss. Max was having the same thoughts, but he came to his senses and pulled away.

"I'm a married man, kid. But I'd be a lucky guy right now if I weren't."

"Hmmm"—she purred with her arms still around him—"why would you be so lucky?"

"I would be in the arms of a beautiful, wonderful woman, and I'd kiss you right here."

"So why don't you? Are you afraid that I'll tattle on you?"

"No, I'm worried that I'd like it, and that wouldn't be fair to you or my wife. You remember her, don't you?"

She said nothing, but her eyes gave him her answer.

"I know this sounds like a line from a bad movie, but you're going to find the right guy one day, one lucky son of a bitch who will make you happy . . . or I'll kill him."

"I thought I had that guy."

He couldn't believe that this beautiful woman wanted him and his eyes started to tear a little. He had a gorgeous wife waiting at home and a beautiful woman in his arms. He kissed her gently on her forehead and gave her a tight squeeze.

"Let's go see what kind of trouble Gino is getting into," he said, and they made their way back to the table.

Gino was having a spirited debate with Gino the waiter about the importance of having anisette with espresso. The waiter was glad to see Max and Sally and quickly took their dessert orders.

"Do you have to start trouble everywhere we go?"

"What do you drink with espresso, sambuca or anisette?"

"I drink anisette."

"There, that proves my point. A place like this had better have anisette, or they need to stop calling it Mario's. They should call it Mel's!"

Max looked over to Sally with a warm smile and patted her hand.

# Chapter Twenty-Five

"**S**on of a BITCH!" Tom screamed into the phone. "They weren't supposed to leave! I don't give a shit about his nose! I paid you to take care of them!

"You mean to tell me that a flat tire is to blame? You had enough time to take care of everything. What do you think the thousand dollars was for?

"What letter? I didn't tell you to give them a letter. What did it say?

"Uh-huh, Milwaukee. The other thousand? Don't worry, you'll get it."

Tom hung up the phone and rubbed his beard.

"Well, Karl, it looks like someone changed our plans."

"What happened?" Karl asked.

"They are on their way to Wisconsin."

"Where is this Wisconsin?"

"It's out in the middle of nowhere. They should be gone another week."

*That would be all right,* Tom thought. He was going to have to deal with the letter writer.

# Chapter Twenty-Six

Max was relieved to be back in New Rochelle after the excitement of the "road trip." He really missed Carol and his own bed and pillow. Sally was asleep in the back, huddled under his overcoat.

"I'm not going to wake her up, Gino. Let her sleep a little more. It goes without saying that I really appreciate your help. Pick me up tomorrow morning, and we'll go to the office. Maybe we can put this together."

"All right, I'll see you at nine," he said.

"Make it eight," Max said, slamming the door and waking Sally.

"We're home? Finally!"

"Sorry to wake you, kid."

"That's okay," she said while stretching. "What do we do now?"

"Now we go home and relax. We'll start fresh in the morning. Be there at eight."

She got out of the car and handed Max his coat. Max took it and gave her a warm smile and patted her cheek.

"Thanks, Sally, for everything. You did a great job, and I'm proud of you."

"You're welcome, boss," she said before giving him a big hug and a kiss on the cheek.

He watched them drive off and couldn't help thinking about their dance. For the first time, he thought about Sally in a romantic way. He had loved her like a little sister, but now that he knew how she felt about him, things were suddenly seen in a different light; if he wasn't a married man, but he was. He loved Carol, and he took an oath. That was where this would have to stop, another time, another place . . .

The front door was unlocked, which was odd. Carol always insisted on locked doors. Entering the living room, he saw Julie doing a crossword puzzle on the couch.

"Welcome back," she said with a little less enthusiasm than he expected. "You're back early."

"Yeah, I cut the trip short. Where is everybody?" he asked while giving his little sister a hug.

"The kids are with Dottie. Carol is upstairs. She's sick."

"What's the matter? She never said anything."

"She's been in bed the last two days. She's been throwing up. She won't eat anything. I offered to call the doctor, but she said not to. She was acting weird the whole time you were gone."

Max ran up the stairs to the bedroom. Carol was awake, but she looked awfully pale.

"Hey, baby, how are you feeling?" Max asked, giving her a kiss on the forehead. "Julie said you were sick."

"What are you doing home?" she asked with a worried look.

"I cut the trip short. You don't look good. What's wrong?"

"Oh, I will be fine. Just let me rest."

"Fine? I don't think so. You're white as a sheet. I'm calling the doctor."

"NO, no, I-I-I am okay."

"Sorry, babe. We'll have the doctor look you over."

Max picked up the receiver of the bedroom phone, and Carol snatched it from his hand.

"Why don't you want me to call—"

"I-I-I . . . I am pregnant!"

Max looked at her with his mouth agape.

"YES!" he shouted and grabbed Carol in a great big hug.

"Ooh," she moaned, and he released his grip on her.

"I'm so sorry, honey. You're having a baby! I'm so happy! When did you find out? Why didn't you tell me?" Max asked with tears already forming in his eyes.

"It was just th-the other day. They said it is normal to feel th-this way."

"Oh my god, right now, I feel anything but normal!"

# Chapter Twenty-Seven

Needless to say this was an occasion for the Chambers family. After telling Julie, Max called everyone he could think of. Mama Chambers yelled so loud that the phone was unnecessary. She organized a quick get-together for the family. Max invited Gino and Sally, and even though they were exhausted from the trip, they came right over. Of course, a quick little get-together for Mama consisted of a feast that could choke a prison. She made a large tray of lasagna and threw together an order of eggplant parmigiana, *bracciole*, meatballs and sausage and peppers. Papa set up a long table in the yard as it was a warm April afternoon and dotted it with his best wine and antipasto and *giardiniera*. Dottie and Julie were hard at work under Mama's orders to help with the food. It was ready within about two hours.

Max almost had to drag Carol out of the bed, but Mama insisted that she come. Some good Italian food was just what she needed to feel better. Mama made a special order of minestrone for her. "They don-na call-a me grandama for not-ing," she said. There were many tears and hugs from the family, and it was just such a happy day. Luckily, Jimmy's funeral was delayed for a couple of days, and Max didn't miss it after all.

As the women cleaned up and prepared desserts, the men relaxed a bit and kept an eye on the kids playing in the yard. Michael and

Stephen were warming up for baseball season and playing catch. Michael was pretty good, but Stephen had a rocket for an arm. He threw hard but was a little wild, giving his brother a workout chasing down the errant throws.

"Holy Jesus, look at the arm on that kid!" Gino exclaimed. "Gus, you better get that kid signed up with the Yankees. He'll give Vic Raschi a run for his money."

"Yup, he's got an arm, but I like the Dodgers. They're gonna have a good team this year. They got Robinson, Reese, and this kid Campanella. Just you watch. I bet they make it the series this year."

"Hey," Papa interrupted, "I don't wanna hear this baseball shit. It's a game for little boys."

"You're right, Pop," Eddie said. "I don't like baseball either."

"Yeah, let's talk about something else," Max said. "Gino, tell that story about when you were in Texas."

"Okay, as long as the women are inside. It was during the war, and I was just out of basic training. They were sending us to the West Coast by train, and we had to stop for a day somewhere in Texas. I don't remember the name of the city. Me and a couple of guys went to this saloon, and it was full of women! I started talking to this one girl and bought her a few drinks to loosen her up.

"She said, 'Let's get out of here and go somewhere where we can be alone.'

"So we started walking, and we got to some woods. We're walking and walking, and finally, we got to a clearing.

"She said, 'Okay, we're here.'

"I said, 'I thought we were going somewhere with a bed!'

"So she said, 'Do you have a handkerchief?'

"I said, 'Yeah?'

"She said, 'Well, spread it out on the ground, and that'll be our bed.'"

"So what did you do?" Eddie asked.

"I took out my handkerchief, you stupid bastard!"

The laughter drowned out the kids and the sound of Carol coming out of the kitchen with a pot of espresso. Everyone had been helping her up and down the porch steps and holding doors for her, but she was alone this time. As she was midway through the seventh or eighth steps to the patio, an errant throw from Stephen sailed her way. She didn't see it coming, and the baseball hit her square in the temple, knocking her unconscious, and down the stairs, she fell.

"Carol!" Max screamed as he saw the fall. Running over to her and cradling her head, he said, "Get some ice over here!"

The family gathered around her as Max put a cold rag to her forehead. Her glasses had broken, and she had a bloody gash on her cheek. He wiped the blood from her face and was relieved that she hadn't been hurt worse, but an ear-piercing scream from Holly alerted everyone to a red stain spreading in the crotch of Carol's gray slacks.

# Chapter Twenty-Eight

The ten-minute ambulance ride to New Rochelle Hospital seemed to take forever to Max as he crouched next to his wife. He watched in horror as a golf-ball-size knot rose on her head. She still hadn't regained consciousness. One of the drivers was in the back with them and had put a bandage on her cheek.

"She's having a baby! Can't you hurry up?"

"Relax, Mr. Chambers. We'll be there in a minute. We're doing all we can."

It seemed to Max that they didn't do anything more than put some gauze on her face and strap her to the stretcher, but he wasn't in the medical field. This was all new to him. He'd never been in an ambulance before. Actually, he didn't remember being in the ambulance that picked him up at Glen Island.

As they wheeled her into the hospital, Max must have said that she was having a baby a dozen times. He wanted to go into the examination room but was gently pushed out and led to the waiting room. Already there were Mama and Papa, Julie and Eddie, Dottie and Gus, and Gino. Sally stayed at the house to watch the kids. Mama was in tears as was Dottie. Everyone else sat or paced in silence. What was there to say? It was a simple accident but could hold dire results.

"Why do they gotta play that fuckin-a shit?" Mama sobbed quietly.

Papa patted her knee gently. "They just-a kids, Francesca. An accident-a."

Max sat in a chair facing the double doors of the room, clutching Carol's purse, knowing she would want her comb and makeup when they finished the examination, while chain-smoking his Lucky Strikes. It was nearly two hours before the doors opened, and Max saw a familiar face, Dr. Maffucci, the family obstetrician. He had delivered Max and his sisters as well as their children.

Max rushed over. "I'm so glad to see you, Doc. Is she okay?"

Much taller than Max with an easy smile and a full head of curly gray hair, he put his arm around Max's shoulder. "Walk with me, Max."

They walked in silence to an empty exam room, and the doctor closed the door.

"Don't tell me this is the big letdown, Doc. How is she?"

"She's going to be fine. She'll have a whopper of a headache, but she'll be fine. She's awake now."

"The baby?"

The doctor paused, taking a deep breath. "I'm sorry, Max. She's not going to have a baby."

"Oh Jesus, I can't believe it."

"The thing is, Max, she's had an abortion, probably two or three days ago. She was bleeding pretty bad, but it didn't have anything to do with today's accident."

Max stared at the doctor, the fog of worry and sadness slowly lifting.

"I assume you didn't know about this."

"Of course, I didn't know about this! What the hell would I know about that kind of shit?"

"I didn't think so. I've known your family almost since I started practicing medicine, so I'm not going to report this. Do you have any idea where she might have gone for this? Would her friends know?"

Realizing he was still clutching Carol's purse, he dumped the contents on the empty table behind him.

"She doesn't have any friends, just my family," Max said as he sifted through the pile. "She's had a rough life, Doc. I've been taking care of her. She has no family left. Just . . ."

Picking a crumpled piece of paper, Max noticed it was from the pad that he kept near the downstairs telephone.

"'Schafer MT Vernon 4-6148.' I don't know who this is."

"I know, Max. William Schafer is a butcher. I took care of some of his 'patients' if you can call them that. They were young girls who probably trusted him even after they paid upfront in cash. They were nearly dead. I didn't press them to file charges because they would have been arrested too. That's who William Schafer is."

Max leaned over the table, holding his cheeks with hands that slowly turned into fists. He closed his eyes, breathing deeply, trying to hold down the rage that was building within.

"Does she know that you can tell that she had this . . . ?"

"Yes. She asked me not to tell you, and I agreed. But I couldn't lie to someone like you. You deserve to know."

"Thanks. Don't let her know that you told me . . . Please, Doctor," Max said in measured tones.

"I won't," Dr. Maffucci said, placing a hand on Max's shoulder, "but don't do anything foolish, to her or anyone else."

"Thank you so much for this. When can I see her?"

"I'll take you there right now."

The color had returned to Carol's face, and she was sitting up in the bed. An IV line snaked from her arm to a bottle of plasma hooked to a pole nearby, and a large ice pack was on her head, held in place by a strip of bandages. The cut on her face had been cleaned and was covered by a small bandage. As soon as she saw Max, she started to weep.

"Hey, baby," Max said softly, "you look like you've been through the mill. Are you okay?"

"Yes, I am okay. Max . . . I-I-I lost th-the baby!"

He closed his eyes and lowered his head. "Oh my god. As long as you're okay, that's all that matters. We can try again. We just have to get you better. That's what's important now."

He hugged her, and they both wept together.

# Chapter Twenty-Nine

There is nothing worse than a funeral of a young man, especially when it's the second time. Jimmy's death in 1945 was a crushing blow to his family, and they had almost come to grips with it. Now seeing the casket and standing in the cemetery made it seem like he had died a second time. His mother was a mess, and his father was able to put forth a stoic front, although he was weeping inside. His brothers and their wives stood around the gravesite with similar expressions of grief and sorrow.

Max stepped forward to deliver the eulogy, and he felt as if he was also saying goodbye to his unborn child. It had only been two days since he heard the horrible news, and his moods alternated from rage to sorrow and finally, to the acceptance of the "event." He looked at the throng of mourners gathered around. Gino was there as was Sally. Max's parents and sisters, sans children, were there. They had watched Jimmy grow up as Max's friend. They couldn't count the number of times he had eaten meals and spent the night at the Chambers's home. It was almost as hard for them as it was for Jimmy's family. Being a Saturday, "Hank" Bernstein wasn't in attendance. He was in the Beth El Temple practicing his religion.

Clearing his throat, Max began, "It's comforting to see so many people here today to say a final goodbye to Jimmy. He was an outgoing person who made a lot of friends. I was lucky enough to be one of them. We grew up together and dealt with the growing pains and joys that are part of life. We made go-carts, stole apples from an unsuspecting neighbor's trees, and went to school together. I can't remember a day spent with him that he didn't suggest some exciting and sometimes foolish adventure for us. We played cowboys and Indians with slingshots that often left us with some pretty big welts that we had to hide from our folks. When there was a heavy rain, we had a tug-of-war over the biggest mudhole we could find. We shot spitballs in class, which we were lucky to get away with because the beatings from our teachers were nothing compared with what our parents would dish out!

"As we got older and started driving, we would all be goaded into hot-rodding around the town. Like I said, if it was exciting or dangerous, Jimmy was all for it and got us to follow along. I think we piled nine people into a car once and were caught speeding. I say 'caught' in the basic sense of the word. Hearing the siren, Jimmy had the bright idea of trying to lose the police. We were on Main Street when we were first spotted, and he must have cut through ten different side streets doing about seventy miles an hour until we wound up at Hudson Park. Instead of blocking the only way in or out, the police followed us into the parking lot. I don't know how we didn't hit someone, but we made a quick circle through the lot and headed back out. Luckily, the cop got stuck behind a car backing out of a space, and we got away. I think that was the LAST time we let him drive!

"Well, the war started, and we were put into some real dangerous situations. We signed up together—Jimmy, Gino Domenico, and I. Jimmy and I were lucky enough to be assigned to the same unit, and we looked out for each other. I've never told anyone this, but he saved my life. To make a long story short, we were in the Hürtgen Forest in Belgium. It was January 1945, and it was a fierce battle. The field was covered in snow, and boy was it cold. It was cold that you can't imagine. Guys were literally freezing to death on both sides. The lucky ones only got frostbite. Well, me and Jimmy were together in a foxhole, and it was the middle of the night. We only had one blanket each, and it was snowing. I finally couldn't take it. I told Jimmy, 'I'm gonna surrender. If I don't, I'm gonna freeze. I'm sorry, but I can't take it anymore.' So I started crawling out of the hole, and he grabbed me and pulled me back in. I was shivering so bad I couldn't get away from him. He started rubbing my arms and legs and lay down on top of me, covering us with the two blankets. I was just about to tell him it was useless when the son of a gun pulls out a flask of brandy! I said, 'What were you holding onto this for, you so and so?' and he said, 'I was waiting till it got cold!' We stayed like that until sunrise, sharing our body heat and sipping the booze, and there was an inch of snow covering us when we stood.

"It was only three months later when Jimmy died. He never knew what hit him, which is a blessing. Unfair is the word that comes to mind when I think that the war was over in a couple of weeks. I often think what if he left five minutes earlier or ten minutes later, if he made a right instead of a left, and it haunted me, but it doesn't change anything. Sadly, Jimmy is now one of the thousands of heroes who saved our country, and we should be proud of him. He loved and respected his parents, loved and respected his brothers and their wives and girlfriends, and he would have been a wonderful husband and father. So let's all say goodbye to Jimmy Kemp. Rest well, my friend."

The priest stepped forward for the final prayer. Father Fleming was a red-faced Irishman with a big nose, probably in his mid-fifties. He mumbled quickly through his services, and Max and his buddies loved working with him when they were altar boys. The masses were usually over in twenty minutes. The "Lord's Prayer" was said, and everyone kneeled and made the sign of the cross. Standing, Max noticed that someone must have come from the temple out of respect. Two bearded gentlemen wearing Hasidic garb also rose and crossed themselves. Rabbi Silverman must have asked them to attend. *That was a very nice gesture,* Max thought.

There is a big difference between an Irish funeral and an Italian funeral. The Italians mourn and cry. The Irish drink and laugh. Max couldn't get over the fun that everyone was having at the reception afterward. It was held at Nicky Kemp's house, and it seemed like a party. Most of the men were drunk within minutes, and there were two young girls doing the Irish Jig. Max made the rounds and paid his respects and made a quick exit. When asked, he answered that Carol was sick in bed and sent her condolences. She was actually still in the hospital, probably for another day or two.

When he got into his car, he didn't know where to go. He didn't feel like going to his empty house, and going to the hospital required a phenomenal amount of restraint. He hadn't told Carol that he knew about her abortion, and he'd have to think carefully about how to bring it up. Driving aimlessly, Max found himself back at the Holy Sepulcher Cemetery again. He parked and wandered back to Jimmy's grave. Surprisingly, tears didn't come. Looking down at the fresh soil, he thought of his aborted child. *Was it a boy or a girl?* he asked himself. *Would it have been a doctor? A lawyer? A housewife? I'll never know . . .*

It wasn't long before he sensed someone close by. It was one of the men from the synagogue whom he'd seen at the funeral. He smiled and nodded at the dark-spectacled man, who nodded in return. He was turning away when he caught a glimpse out of the corner of his eye. The Jewish man knelt in front of a stone crucifix marker and made the sign of the cross. *Jews don't do that,* Max thought and then remembered that the two Jewish men had done the same at the funeral.

Max strolled over to the man. "I'd like to thank you for attending the funeral today."

The man nodded.

"My name is Max," he said, offering his hand to the man.

The man nodded again and shook Max's hand.

He couldn't see the man's eyes through the dark glasses he wore. It was getting dark now. Most people would have taken off their sunglasses by now.

"Can you see all right?" Max asked as he quickly snatched the dark glasses from the man's face and was jolted back in time.

Max found himself looking into a pair of cold gray eyes full of hatred and evil. They were the eyes that he'd seen most nights in his nightmares. They were the eyes of Karl Schmitt.

"I know you, you murdering son of a b—" Max said before he was punched hard in the gut by Schmitt. Then he heard the CRACK and smelled the gunpowder and realized that he'd been shot. It knocked the wind out of him. He staggered back until he was leaning on a large gravestone. He watched Karl Schmitt turn and quickly walk away.

NO, Max thought and drew his .45, firing at him but missing, hitting a stone. Schmitt ducked behind a marker and fired back, hitting the stone just above Max's shoulder. Max quickly ducked forward, lying behind a gravestone that chipped when struck by another bullet from the German.

"I'm sorry," Max said, looking at the marker, "Caruso John and Leslie." He checked the wound in his side. It didn't hurt. *I must be in shock,* he thought. It wasn't bleeding as much as he thought it would. The close range of the shot had practically cauterized it. He rolled over and hid behind a different stone, which was chipped by another German bullet. "I'm sorry again, Salvino Lewis and Rosalie."

Getting into a crouch, Max made a zigzag run across a row of graves, diving for cover. He immediately rose and fired a shot, which struck the German, knocking him backward to the ground. Max ran forward and stopped for cover and took off again five seconds later. No shots had been fired since he hit the German, so he ran toward him in a crouch, ready to fire. Schmitt was on his back, blood coming from a wound in his shoulder. A luger was about ten feet behind him. Max picked the smoking gun with his left hand; his right was pointing his .45 at the fallen man.

Max stood over his fallen foe. "Greetings," he said, still pointing his pistol.

"I surrender . . . No need for more shooting," Schmitt said with a heavy accent. He began to stand.

"Don't get up on my account," Max said quietly as he fired a shot into his ankle.

"AHHH, I surrender! Don't shoot!"

"You surrender?"

"Yes! Call the police! I will go quietly!"

"No, I don't think so. Let's keep this between us," he said in an even tone as he fired another shot into the German's kneecap.

"AHHH!"

"All those people—women, children, old people—you killed them like rats. You killed my friend. You disgusting parasite, after all you did at those camps, you have the brass balls to dress as a Jew!"

"I did not kill him! Tom—"

"Don't interrupt me." Another shot hit the Nazi in the thigh.

"Aaahh! It was Tom's idea! Tom Dekarry. He is my partner. I will tell you where to find him!"

"Why would I want him?"

"There is gold! Diamonds! A fortune! Let me live, and you can have it all!"

"Let me live . . . How often did you ignore that plea when you were shoving them in the gas chambers?"

"It was orders! I was just a soldier!"

"I was a soldier. My pal was a soldier. You were a murderer." Max fired a shot into his other shoulder.

"Oooohh," he moaned. "I am sorry! I will do anything!"

"It's too late to do anything that I care about. Where's your partner?"

"2844 Union Turnpike in Queens. Now please call for a doctor!"

He heard the sirens. "I don't think a doctor's gonna get here in time . . .," he said, feeling light-headed and firing another shot, smashing the German's other knee. "Wait, I just thought of something you can do."

His face lit up. "Anything! I will do anything!"

"Go straight to fucking hell, you Nazi motherfucker!"

Max emptied his pistol into Karl Schmitt's body and watched as the life went out of his eyes. The sirens were getting closer, and Max backed up and leaned against a large gravestone. He slowly sank to the ground, tossing the luger onto Karl Schmitt's lifeless body. Max fumbled in his pockets and pulled out his cigarettes. Taking a deep drag, he looked up at the darkening sky. He felt his warm blood oozing down his belly and saw the stain spreading.

"This was my good suit," he said aloud with a chuckle. "I got him, Jimmy!" He started to fall over into the fresh mowed grass. *I guess I won't have to go far,* he thought as his head hit the ground. More sirens were wailing. It was getting dark, very dark . . . until there was nothing but blackness.

# Chapter Thirty

"**Y**'know, these goddamned bureaucrats are ruining the country! All they want to talk about are Communists!"

Gino's rant startled Max as he was reading the *NY Daily News* in his hospital bed. He did this from time to time, and Max found it easier to just grunt in agreement. Gino loved a good debate and often took the opposing side just to keep things going. Max smiled and shook his head at his buddy's antics. He had saved Max's hide after the shooting in the cemetery. He raced to New Rochelle Hospital with "Hank" Bernstein and the dossier on Karl Schmitt when the police were preparing to charge Max with murder. The family was getting all too used to the waiting room, and they kept a vigil until Max was out of surgery, and it was deemed he would be fine. Amazingly, the bullet had missed any major organ and came out his back. He needed blood badly, but aside from that, he was awake and lucid as he spoke with the family a few hours later. The police were told to come back the next day.

Max was sitting up in his bed, reading the paper that Gino had brought. He'd shown up with every paper that was sold in New Rochelle and some good coffee and sat with Max in the early morning hours. The detectives who arrived were familiar faces. Bob Flaherty and Jack McCarthy had gone to school with them.

"Well, if it isn't two members of the Hitler Youth paying me a visit! Gino, look, do you remember these guys?"

Gino looked up from his paper. "Yup." He quickly looked back to the paper as he also had no use for them.

"How are your old men? Are they still proud Bundists?"

Both of their fathers had been vocal members of the American Nazi Party otherwise known as the German American Bund. One of them, Max couldn't remember which, actually had a key chain with a silver swastika hanging from it. Their sons were members in waiting when they were drafted and, ironically, were sent to Europe to fight the Nazis. The fathers hung their heads in shame when they realized the Bund's true intentions, and their sons were put in harm's way.

"All right, enough with the cracks. Let's talk about the guy you murdered two nights ago."

"Where the hell have you guys been? Your captain was here already and got all the evidence."

"Yeah, but I still want to know why you didn't tell us that you were chasing a Nazi in our town."

"I'm a private investigator. Pay close attention to the word 'private.' If my client wanted you to know, he would have let you know, you half-baked Nazi pigs. Get the fuck out of my room!"

"Oh, tough guy, huh? How about a little tune-up to loosen your tongue?"

Gino stood, waving his arms over his head. "Hey, why don't you get the hell outta here? Go talk to your captain, you stupid bastards!"

McCarthy took a step toward him when Max yelled, "Hey! You wanna be tough, guys? I'll take youse both on! It's two to one, and I'm in a hospital bed, so it'll be your idea of a fair fight!"

The shouting brought Nurse Adious into the room. "Gentlemen, this is no place for shouting. Mr. Chambers has suffered a severe injury and should not be disturbed. Please leave, or I will call your superiors."

The two detectives looked at each other and thought otherwise about their intentions. Two other men entered the room.

"We're with the state department. What are you two flatfoots doing here?"

"We're conducting an investigation," Flaherty said with a suddenly respectful tone.

"No, you're not," said one of the new visitors as they flashed their badges. "We've taken over the case. Get out of here, or I'll have you checking parking meters for the rest of your lives."

The detectives slowly left the crowded room.

"Gentlemen, Mr. Chambers needs his rest. I can't allow anyone getting him excited," the nurse said.

"We won't be any trouble. We just have a few questions, and we'll leave him alone."

That seemed to satisfy Nurse Adious, and she moved to Max's bed and gently fluffed his pillow. Her face broke into what could be generously described as a smile as she looked at him. She had lost family members in the Holocaust as had millions of others and was proud to be caring for Max.

"Mr. Chambers is a hero. You should treat him as such," she said as she left the room.

Max literally shuddered as he thought of Nurse "Hideous" and her creepy smile.

"I'm Agent Harold, and this is Agent Stevens. We'd like to talk about what happened if you're up to it," said the tall man as they both removed their hats.

"Sure, pull up a chair. I'm not going anywhere."

"We'd like to know how you were able to find that Nazi here in New Rochelle. I thought they were all hiding in South America," he said, offering cigarettes to Max and Gino.

Max told them the story from the beginning, leaving out how he'd been "coerced" into it. They knew most of what he told them as they had taken all the evidence from the local police and made a beeline to the address in Queens, but Tom Dekarry was long gone. Agents were dispatched to the safe houses and to Red's Roadhouse.

Agent Stevens would sit watch at Max's room in the event of any foul play by the missing Tom Dekarry.

"I'm a little surprised to see the state department here," Max said. "Bernstein said that you didn't want anything to do with this."

Taking a deep drag, Agent Harold said, "I know, but we thought he was just some crackpot. We got egg on our faces from that, all right. I understand your wife is also here. We're placing an agent at her room too. When you or your wife are released, we'll have a round-the-clock watch at your house, just in case."

"I don't think that's necessary," Max said as his mood darkened at the thought of Carol and what she had done.

"I don't think so either, but it's just to be on the safe side. Listen, you earned whatever you charged for killing that bastard."

"Yeah," Agent Stevens said with a chuckle. "The lousy Nazi looked like Swiss cheese! I heard they were having trouble embalming him with all the holes you drilled him with!"

"We're going to leave you alone now, and I hope you get out of here soon but PLEASE notify us if you get any info on this other guy."

They shook hands all around, and the two agents left. The room was eerily quiet, and Max's thoughts went back to Carol.

# Chapter Thirty-One

I t was time to go home, and Max was relieved. He had been in the hospital for ten long days, and it was an ordeal. The place was deathly quiet, and his visitors were constantly told to lower their voices. Aside from reading the papers with Gino in the mornings, most of his visitors had been banned from the hospital. Mama was turned away with a steaming plate of ziti.

"Mr. Chambers is a sick man and can't have any of that unhealthy food," she was told by "warden" Adious.

She was told in less than quiet tones, "Unhealthy! *Che tu puoi essere mangiato da I cano to sei cosa brutta!*" You should be eaten alive by dogs, you ugly thing!

Eddie and his trusty flask were next after Nurse "Hideous" noticed the alcohol on Max's breath. Dottie was caught bringing in a prosciutto sandwich in her purse. Julie almost made it through with a bottle of ginger ale filled with scotch. The staff did everything but check his stool and sniff his farts to make sure he only ate the hospital food, if one could call it that.

So Max was ready to leave. He took walks up and down the corridor to build up his strength. His wound was healed, and stitches were removed by a doctor, reminding him to take everything slow and easy for a month or so, but he had another idea in mind.

Slowly easing back into the front seat of Gino's car, Max said, "Let's take a little detour. I'd love to see Mount Vernon."

"Is there any particular reason that you need to see it today?"

"Y'know, yeah, but you'll know as soon as we get there."

"I will?"

"Yeah. I'm gonna need you there in case I have a relapse."

"I hate when you keep me in the dark," Gino said, shaking his head.

Max patted his shoulder. "It's important, buddy. I just can't talk about it right now, okay?"

"Don't worry about it. I'm getting used to this second-class treatment," he said with a smile.

Number 863 Fourth Street was a fairly nondescript building with assorted offices. Max and Gino walked around the back to an alley with a back door. They walked up tree flights and entered room 306. Max locked the door as Gino looked on in surprise.

"Dr. Schafer! Dr. Schafer!" Max called out.

Dr. William Schafer entered the reception area from the other room of the dingy small office. He was a weasel-looking bastard with a bald head and a hooked nose.

"Yes, I'm Dr. Schafer. I think you may have the wrong Dr. Schafer. I happen to be an obstetrician."

"You're the right one," Max said as he immediately punched the small older man in the face. His little body rolled over the reception desk like a rag doll. Moving quickly, Max grabbed him by his shirt and pulled him up, delivering another hard blow to face, knocking him through the doorway of his exam room. Schafer slid on the waxed floor until his bald head slammed into the far wall.

"I'd like to talk about one of your patients!" Max growled as he stood over the fallen doctor. "Do you remember Carol Chambers?" he said, delivering a kick to the little man's side.

"Wait, wait, wait!" He panted. "I only did what she asked!"

Max lifted him to his feet. "You mean you aborted her baby. Why don't you speak plain English, you butcher?" Max punched him as hard as he could in his weakening state and watched Schafer flip over the exam table. He was breathing hard, and his side ached, but he was moving on pure instinct as he grabbed the table and flipped it over. Picking Schafer, he said, "You're leaving town. TODAY!" He punctuated it with a slap across the bleeding man's face. "I'll be back here tomorrow!" SLAP. "I'm gonna do the same thing!" SLAP. "You won't call the cops because they'll send you to prison for twenty years!" SLAP. "I'll do this tomorrow!" SLAP. "And the next day!" SLAP. "And every fucking day that I see you!" SLAP. "Do I make myself clear?" PUNCH.

Schafer sunk to the floor, whimpering, "I'll go . . . Please don't hit me. I'll go."

Max turned to walk away but changed his mind. "I thought you'd see it my way!" With that, he delivered a vicious kick to the bleeding William Schafer's face, knocking him cold.

Holding his side, Max quickly turned and walked through the door, passing a shocked Gino. "Let's go," he huffed, "or do you wanna put your feet in the stirrups?"

Gino quietly closed the door behind him and followed Max down the stairs to the car. Neither of them spoke for a minute. Max was slowly catching his breath and holding his aching side. The knuckles on his right hand were bleeding and hurt like hell. Gino had his hands on the wheel of the parked car, staring ahead. He reached over and put his hand on Max's head, brushing the hair from his forehead gently, and put Max's hat on his head. He still had no idea what to say.

Max leaned over and gave Gino a hug and kissed his cheek, Italian style. "Now you know. You're the only one who knows."

Gino silently nodded.

"And now you know why I don't want to go home. Let's go to the office."

He silently nodded and started the car.

# Chapter Thirty-Two

S ally practically jumped when she saw Max. "What are you doing here, you big jerk? You're supposed to be resting!"

She gave him a big hug, and he returned it. Things had changed between them. He realized how much he cared for her and her for him. Carol had broken his heart, and he didn't know if he could ever forgive her for what she had done.

"I missed you, kid," he said and gave her a quick kiss on the lips. She melted in his arms.

"Oh, Max . . ." She quickly snapped out of the moment and said, "The phones have been ringing off the hook. The *New York Times* called, the Associated Press. They all want to talk to you. The television stations want to put you on the news—"

"I'm not in! I don't care if Truman calls! I'm not in!"

Gino closed the door behind them as Max took a seat behind his desk. The bottom drawer held an unopened bottle of Chivas Regal, a gift from Eddie.

"This is as good a time any. Whaddaya say, Gino?"

"Oh jeez, it's 10:00 a.m.!"

"I guess that's a yes. Sally, could you come in here for a minute?"

She rushed into the office as he was pouring three glasses. "What are we drinking to?"

"Dead Nazis."

"Gimme a glass."

They clinked their glasses together and shot back the fiery liquid. The phone rang in the outer office, and Sally rushed out, closing the door behind her.

The shot didn't help, so Max poured another round, offering one to Gino, who held up a hand.

"Not right now."

Max shrugged and poured the contents into his glass.

"Hey, maybe you ought to take it easy on that. You're not gonna be in any shape—"

"Shape to what? I've already beaten up all the doctors I planned to!"

"It's just . . . I'm really sorry about . . . everything."

"Thanks, buddy," Max said as he shot back to remains of his drink.

"Why did she . . . ?"

"I don't know. I can't bring myself to talk to her about it. I'm so confused. I'm pissed. I'm so pissed! I want to . . . have another drink!"

He quickly filled a glass and shot it back.

"Max, Mr. Bernstein is here to see you," Sally said over the intercom.

Yelling into the machine, he said, "I'm not in! Tell him I went to Wonderland!"

The office door opened, and "Hank" Bernstein walked in, followed by Sally.

"I'm sorry, Max. I told him he couldn't—"

"Good morning, Max. Please don't blame Ms. Connors. Sometimes I can be very, how do you say, pushy."

"It's okay, Sally. Leave us alone for a minute, please."

She backed out and closed the door.

"Hank, you picked a rotten fucking time to pay me a visit!"

"Yes, I would love to sit. Ah, scotch, thank you. I would love some."

He poured himself a glass and nodded toward Gino as he took a sip.

"Mr. Domenico, I hope you are well."

"Well? Well . . ."

Max was leaning back in his chair, glass in hand. He gave "Hank" an evil stare.

"I got Schmitt. The case is over as far as I'm concerned, or have you found another reason to blackmail me?"

"Max, you must not take things so seriously."

"I took a fucking bullet! That's serious!"

"Yes, I know. Karl Schmitt was an evil man, but you knew that. Anyway, there is a reward for the capture of Schmitt, and you captured him."

Max raised his eyebrows and looked at his partner as "Hank" dug into his worn leather briefcase and pulled out some files. Gino was licking his lips and smiling like a Cheshire cat while rubbing his palms together. Max couldn't help but smile at his antics.

"Now the reward was for his capture, dead or alive. I am happy to say that you have earned $25,000. Here is a bank draft made payable to Max Chambers."

"That's all right, we'll split it up later," Gino said with a smile that wouldn't fade.

Max looked at the check. He couldn't believe that he was holding that much money in his hands. *Is it enough?* he thought. *Is it enough for all I'd been through, for what Gino and Sally had been through? If I hadn't been driving around the country, I might have stopped Carol from getting the abortion, just maybe.*

"Now," "Hank" said, bringing Max back to reality, "I have identified the last member of the group that Karl Schmitt led. Here is a picture. It was very hard for me to get ahold of, but I finally got it."

He shoved it toward Max. "Her name is Elsa Burkhardt. She was a guard at Buchenwald."

Max picked the photo. She was a fairly attractive woman, unsmiling, with braided blond hair. He looked at "Hank" with a shrug.

"Do you have any idea of her whereabouts?"

"A little. Let me show you something," "Hank" said, taking back the photo. He rummaged through his briefcase and took out a carpenter pencil. After unwrapping the tip, he sharpened it with a small penknife.

"You see, Max," he said while scribbling on the photo, "a person can change the hairstyle, change the color, and she becomes a new woman. If she wears glasses, it makes a distinct change." He finished his scribbling on the photo. "There, does she look familiar now?"

Max picked the photo. IT WAS CAROL.

He practically jumped from his seat and grabbed Hank by his lapels, pulling him across the desk.

"You fucking bastard! How dare you accuse my wife—"

"Max, please just look at the photo!"

"You knew this all along and said nothing?"

"I did not! I went to visit you at home, and she answered the door. It was when you were in Virginia. I did not realize it until later."

Gino pried Max off Hank and got in the middle. "Just calm down. It can't be her," he said as he picked the photo. *But it is her,* he thought as his eyes widened.

Max moved to the office window and looked out over New Rochelle. He closed his eyes and thought back to that horrible day at Buchenwald.

*There weren't any women, wait, there were a few. After they loaded the guards on the truck, a line of female guards was led out. They walked like women, any women. They shook their hips and walked on shapely legs. NO, not all of them, ONE of them. She had a body like Ann Sheridan! O dear God in heaven, that was Carol! I am a private investigator who married a Nazi! It is almost funny! How could I have been so blind?*

"Max, you must believe me. I had no idea that Elsa Burkhardt was part of this. It was only after I saw her in your home."

Max sat at the desk and buried his face in his hands. "That's why she stammers, right?"

"Germans have great difficulty pronouncing the 'th' sounds and the 'w' sounds among others. It was evident within minutes of speaking with her that she was hiding a German accent."

*So that's why I have those nightmares,* he thought. *That's why I can't get rid of that smell, that atrocious odor from Buchenwald. I've been sleeping with it all these years! I've made love it! Love? Who am I in love with? It's not with Carol, and it's not with Elsa Burkhardt. I've been a fucking dope!*

Sally came into the office after hearing the ruckus. "Is everything okay?"

"Yes, everything is just hunky dory! My wife is a Nazi! Maybe I should put that on my business cards. That'll really instill confidence in a client!"

She picked the photo, and as her eyes widened, she slowly shook her head. She didn't say anything, which surprised Max. Gino was also taken aback by her silence.

"Oh yeah, I forgot to tell you. She didn't lose the baby. She had an abortion! That's why she was bleeding at the party. She went to a butcher while we were on a wild-goose chase! She's part of the gang that we've been following!"

He poured himself another drink and lit a cigarette. The room was silent. Hank was straightening his jacket, Gino was pacing with his hands in his pockets, and Sally was staring at Max. She slowly walked behind his chair and gave him a tender hug. He reached back and patted her curly blond head.

"So what's the deal with Elsa Burkhardt? I'm gonna go out on a limb and guess that she wasn't just a typist. What's her story?"

Hank sat back and picked his files. He took a deep breath. "She was a brutal guard. I have witnesses who have seen her beat people to death with a truncheon. She walked around with a vicious dog and ordered it to attack at the slightest infraction. She is directly responsible for fourteen murders."

Max closed his eyes again and tried to imagine his meek and mild wife beating people to death. How could he have been so blind?

He thought back to the pub in London where they first met. She was talking with someone and pointing at him. All that bumping into each other was all part of her plan. He was the mark. He wasn't any great Casanova; she seduced him. It was all mapped out, right down to the quickie wedding. The real Carol Bird was dead somewhere in Europe, killed by the woman he was going to spend his life with. Why? Why was he so important? What did he have to do with their plan? She could have escaped once they got stateside, but she didn't. So that wasn't it. He couldn't figure it out. Maybe it was all the booze, but his head was spinning.

"I think I need to go home," he said, standing suddenly on unsteady legs. "I wanna hear what my wife has to say about all this. Gino, can you give me a ride?"

"Sure," he said.

"Close up the office, Sally. Go home and stay there. In fact, we'll take you home. You too, Hank. C'mon, let's leave right now. Everybody, stay at your homes until you hear from me."

# Chapter Thirty-Three

Max was drunk when he walked through his front door. Dottie and her husband were sitting on the couch, while Michael and Stephen were wrestling on the floor. Peter was sitting in his playpen.

"Good morning, one and all!"

Everyone rushed to him. The boys gave him a rough hug, nearly knocking him over. Carol tried to give him a big hug, but he brushed her off to greet his sister.

"We were worried about you," Dottie said. "The hospital said that you were released. Where the hell did you go?"

"I had to stop by the office."

"You smell like you stopped by a bar."

"Strictly for medicinal purposes, Dot."

Carol was holding on to his arm as he made his way to his favorite chair. A fire was crackling in the fireplace. She knelt next to him, still holding his arm.

"You should have come straight home instead of th-the office."

"Yeah, I shouldn't have gone to the office. That's for sure," he said, shooting a glare at Carol. "Why don't you and the kids take off? I'm just gonna go to bed and get some sleep. That's the one thing they won't let you do at the hospital."

Dottie packed up the boys and left within a few minutes. One of the state department agents was sitting in his car in front of the house. He waved at Max.

The house was suddenly deathly quiet, and Max made his way up to the bedroom. Carol followed closely behind. She was folding down the bed covers for Max.

"Can I get you something to eat?"

"No."

"Okay."

"Sprechen sie deutch, Elsa?"

"Ja-w-what?" she asked with a startled expression.

"I'm sorry, did I say Elsa? Elsa Burkhardt was a brutal, murderous Nazi guard at Buchenwald. I was given a file on her today, and her photo looks just like you. Isn't that a coincidence?"

"W-what photo?"

Max took the scribbled-on photo out of his jacket pocket and shoved it at Carol.

"Does she look like anyone you know?"

Carol's face paled as she saw the photo. She said nothing.

"Oh, I forgot to tell you. I have a new doctor. His name is Schafer. Does that name ring a bell?"

Their eyes met, and the charade was over. Max grabbed Carol's shoulders and shook her like a rag doll. He gave her a hard slap across the face, which knocked her to the floor.

"That's for aborting my child! You murdered my child! WHY? Is it because you're a fucking Nazi? You murdered innocent people at that death camp, and you murdered my baby!"

She scrambled to her feet and ran downstairs, but Max was right behind her. He caught up to her in the living room and gave her another vicious slap across the face, knocking her down again.

"That's for Buchenwald! You were working with Karl Schmitt! I was nearly killed, and you were working with him? You had me driving around the middle of nowhere! I was supposed to be killed in Virginia, wasn't I? What comes next?"

She ran to the kitchen, and he followed her. She turned to face him, clutching a large knife.

"So that's what comes next. Why didn't you just kill me in my sleep? You could have saved so much time!"

"I did not want you killed! That is why I had them send you to Milwaukee!" she said without a hint of a stammer as she threw the photo into the fireplace.

"'Vat' is 'sa' matter?" he asked in a mocking German accent. "Have you forgotten your stammer? I guess it doesn't matter now anyway!"

"What are you going to do?"

"That's a good question. Maybe I'll call the agent inside and tell him the whole story. They'll probably laugh in my face. After all, who would be so stupid as to marry a Nazi and never figure it out?"

"Max, I love you! I was just supposed to stay with you for a little while, but I fell in love with you! I could never have had them hurt you!"

"You're breaking my heart," he said with a laugh. "I guess Hans never got the memo!"

"Hans was just supposed to take the girl to the safe house in Elkridge, and you were supposed to follow him there!"

"What would I find there, her dead body?"

"No, she was not to be killed. You were supposed to follow the clues to Virginia to keep you out of town!"

"What was happening in town that I wasn't supposed to see?"

Her mouth opened, but she said nothing. Her eyes looked to the floor. It was that moment that made him realize that there was no love between them. She wouldn't tell him the plans, even though her true identity was now known. Max looked at her with a mixture of sadness and regret and a wave of revulsion came over him. He turned and made his way upstairs to retrieve his pistol. It was in his hand as he came back down the steps.

"Don't worry, I'm not gonna shoot you. You already destroyed my life so far, but you're not gonna destroy the rest of it."

He put on his hat and coat and walked out the door.

# Chapter Thirty-Four

"**G**ino, you must help me! I am worried about Max!"

Gino took a deep breath as he spoke into the phone. "I wouldn't worry about Max. Besides, I probably shouldn't be talking to you."

"I am not that person in the photo! I am sure he showed it to you, but he is wrong!"

Gino said nothing.

"He said he was thinking of killing himself! He said he was going to Hudson Park, but he should have been home by now. Could you please meet me there?"

Gino didn't understand the logistics of what she'd said, but he knew Max was drunk when he last saw him. "Okay, I'll meet you there. Wait, how are you getting there?"

"Don't worry, I'll be there," she said, hanging up the phone.

He arrived at the entrance to Hudson Park in about fifteen minutes, and Carol was standing on the top step. Getting out of his car, he called out, "How'd you get here?"

Ignoring his query, she said, "I think I saw him over there. Come quickly!"

She grabbed his hand and pulled him through the park, rushing to a hilltop overlooking the beach. It was getting dark, and the park was empty.

"I don't see anyone," he said, looking around. The hilltop offered a vantage point of the entire park and empty beach.

"Oh, I don't know what to do," Carol said, giving Gino a hug. "You don't believe that I'm a Nazi, do you?"

"It's not important what I believe right now. We're trying to find Max."

Carol hugged him tighter, almost in a sexual way. He spread his arms out wide and tried to pull away when he heard a click followed by a sharp pinch. It wasn't a pinch. He realized too late as the knife plunged deep into his belly. He futilely tried to pull away, but Carol had a firm grip on him. He breathlessly moaned as she sliced him from his navel around to his spine. He sunk to his knees as she released her grip on him, and he fell over on his side.

"You Nazi bitch," he whispered, trying to hold his guts from spilling out.

"I'm sorry, Gino," she said, folding back the switchblade. "We were all going to disappear, but you found out too much. Goodbye."

She hurried quickly to the waiting car and took one last look to make sure that Gino was dead. She smiled when she saw his body stop moving and got into the car. She had one more stop to make.

# Chapter Thirty-Five

After leaving his house, Max drove aimlessly around town before finally stopping at Glen Island Park, just a few blocks from home. As he sat in the sand, different thoughts raced through his mind, but there was just too much to decipher. The woman he'd loved didn't even exist. Even worse, she was an escaped Nazi who was involved with the group that tried to kill him. Add to that the fact that she was a brutal guard at Buchenwald who had murdered fourteen people. Plus, she had aborted their child. He literally shook his head so much that he was getting a sore neck. Finally, he decided the next course of action. She would have to face justice. He would tell the whole story to the State Department people. When they stopped laughing in his face, they would take Carol, no, Elsa to the proper place for her trial. He still wasn't sure if he'd stand by her side, but she would definitely stand trial. He made his way back to the parking lot. It was dark now.

He gave a wave to the agent parked across the street and entered his house. All the lights were off, except for upstairs. As he turned on the lamp in the living room, a voice called out, "Oh, Maxie! Maxie baby!" He knew the voice.

"Come upstairs, Maxie baby!"

He dropped his coat and hat on the couch and followed the familiar voice up the stairs. Carol was held with a gun to her head by a man with a face he didn't know.

"You took long enough to get here, Maxie baby!" the man said in a singsong patter. He was right about the voice. It was the voice of Jimmy Kemp.

"Jimmy? Is that really you?"

"Yeah, it's really me. Now drop the gun slowly."

Max slowly took out his pistol and placed it on the floor.

"Kick it over here."

He did so.

"How . . . how . . . how?"

"You haven't lost your gift of gab," Jimmy said with a high-pitched giggle.

"But . . . but . . ."

"Y'know, she's supposed to stutter, not you!"

"You were killed!"

"I'll tell you what, stop saying shit like that, and I'll tell you what happened. Y'see, while I was rousting Karl Schmitt and his boys out of that guardhouse, he made me a wonderful proposal. He told me about the shitload of gold and diamonds that he stashed away and offered to share it with me if I let him go. So I said okay. So when I drove the truck far enough away, we killed everyone and set it on fire. The explosion and the extra gasoline burned everything. All we had to do was switch around some dog tags."

"Was Frazier in on this too?"

"No, you see, Frazier didn't have quite a forward-thinking mentality, so he had to go."

"I see you've got a new face."

"Yeah, plastic surgery. I look a little like Cary Grant now."

"You shaved your beard."

"Yeah, a beard like that is only good for a rabbi. Or maybe a pirate. Yeah, I could be Jew-beard the Pirate!"

"Jimmy, don't do this. We were like brothers."

"Bullshit Max! You sold me out every chance you got in the war. I should have gotten those promotions! I should have gotten those medals! The one chance you had to help me out was sending me away in that truck!"

"Then what about your family? They're heartbroken. Did you think of them?"

"To hell with my rotten family and to hell with you Max. I'm going to be an international playboy. I've seen how the other half lives and I love it."

"You prick," Max said as the anger built up inside him. "I was doing all this to somehow avenge your death."

"Yeah well, as usual you're coming up short. I'm sticking with my plan."

"Well, why are you holding a gun on Elsa? She's part of your gang, isn't she?"

"She is, but she didn't want to see you get hurt, so I'm not taking any chances till it's over."

"How does everything become 'over'?"

"That's a good question. I'm glad you asked. You and your wife are going to be found dead in your bed after they put out the fire set by a vengeful Tom Dekarry. That's a funny story. I told Schmitt not to call me Jimmy. Call me Tom, Dick, or Harry. The stupid Kraut thought I said Tom Dekarry, and it stuck! Anyway, while they're putting out the fire, I'll be digging up Jimmy's grave. That's where all the loot has always been! They went and put a guard at the cemetery in Germany just as we were about to dig it up, so we had to wait. Pretty good plan, huh?"

"Jimmy—"

"Now don't start with the 'why did you do it?' I told you a thousand times I was looking for gold or glory. I didn't get the glory, but boy have I got the gold!"

"How are you going to get Elsa to hop into bed with me while you burn down my house?"

"It isn't gonna be Elsa. It's gonna be that dumb secretary of yours. She should be here any minute. Elsa said you were gonna kill yourself. First, we kill you two. Then we start the fire."

"You're going to kill that kid?"

"I'll kill whoever gets in my way! By the way, you have got to be the worst private eye in history. Who brings their fucking secretary on a job?" Jimmy said with his high-pitched giggle.

"There's only one problem. If you fire that gun, the agent across the street will be here in a flash," Max said.

"That agent is dead. We got him as soon as it got dark. Elsa shook her hips to distract him, while I slit his throat."

"What are you going to do about the guards at the cemetery? They know all about the loot, and they're waiting for Tom Dekarry," Max lied.

For the first time, Jimmy's smile faded. "When did they post guards?"

"This afternoon. Where do you think I went after I left here? I told them about Elsa, and Bernstein figured out the loot was in the grave," Max said with a smile.

"Well, you're gonna get rid of 'em. We're going there now."

"Not a chance, Jimmy."

No sooner did the words leave Max's mouth than he heard pounding at the front door. It was Sally.

"You'll take a ride with me, while your secretary stays here with Elsa."

Max took the only chance he was ever going to get and made a move toward Jimmy and the gun. He wasn't going to let Sally fall into their hands even if it killed him. Max got his hand on the barrel and twisted, breaking Jimmy's finger, but stumbled in the scuffle and lost his grip. He fell to the floor on the landing. It was when Jimmy switched hands that Elsa made her move. Using her switchblade once again, she stabbed Jimmy deep in his gut and pulled the knife upward into his chest. Jimmy dropped the gun and fell to the floor, gurgling on the blood in his throat. Max dove for the gun, but Elsa was too close and too fast.

"Don't do this. Don't kill anymore. I'll stand by your side like I have all these years. I'll tell them about Jimmy, about how you were forced to do this. They'll go easier on you," Max said from the floor.

"Easier? How much easier? They'll put me on display and tell lies about me! I was just a girl when they forced me to be a guard! I had no choice then, and I have no choice now! I had no choice but to kill Jimmy's baby! It wasn't yours, Max. I loved you, Max, but it's too late now."

"It's not too late," Max pleaded. "Let me help you. You said you loved me, now trust me. We'll tell them your story and they'll understand. They will-"

"Understand? They will hang me from a rope and take pictures of me! They will call me names like those other women! Is that how they will understand? I will go the way I want to go!"

Max yelled, "NO!" but it was drowned out by the gunshot that burst through Elsa's head, and she dropped to the floor. It was all too obvious that she was dead, and Max bowed his head. He heard a crash from the kitchen and realized Sally had broken the glass of his back door. She came running up the stairs and saw Max rising to his feet.

Realizing that he was all right, she practically flew into his arms. "I heard a shot, Max! I was so worried!"

Still holding her, Max said, "Sally, meet Jimmy, also known as Tom Dekarry."

# Chapter Thirty-Six

"Y'know, these goddamned bureaucrats are ruining this country," Gino said from his hospital bed while reading the newspaper. "All they want to do is hunt for commies."

Luckily, Elsa and Tom/Jimmy had driven off before he'd been able to get to his feet. There was no one around to help him, so he drove himself to the hospital. He lay on his side as the other was stitched, about a hundred stitches. He also saved having to pay for an ambulance ride.

Max had just gotten there with Hank Bernstein and fresh coffee and newspapers. There had been a big write-up in the papers nationwide over what happened. Max's poor wife had been killed when evil Tom Dekarry showed up at the house, looking for revenge. She managed to mortally wound him before he shot her in the head. The agent killed in his car had also been killed by Dekarry. Using tremendous intuition, Bernstein had deduced that something could be hidden in Jimmy's grave. So under cover of night, Jimmy Kemp was exhumed, and a huge cache of gold bullion and diamonds was discovered in his casket. He was reburied without mention. Gino had been "mugged" at Hudson Park and nearly killed. He told the authorities that he'd been mistaken for a drug dealer, and when he didn't have the drugs, he was viciously knifed. The assailant had gotten away.

"Our story is on page 5 now," Max said. "It looks like we're old news."

"Yeah, three weeks later and we're all but forgotten."

"Say, how long are you gonna milk this little scratch for?"

"Yeah, just remember it was your wife who put me here. Next time, you gotta marry an Italian. I hear they're nice and quiet."

Max smiled at the comment. He couldn't help but smile. It hadn't taken him long to come to grips with his wife's subterfuge. He realized that he wasn't in love with a real person. Those first nights when he found himself missing Carol, he was reminded that Carol was really Elsa Burkhardt, a murderer and a vicious Nazi who did anything to keep up her charade. Together, he and Gino had "stumbled" through the case and foiled the plan of the evil Nazis. Carol Bird Chambers was laid to rest, and Max thought it was appropriate that she finally had a tombstone. Who knew whatever became of her remains? Elsa Burkhardt remained on the "wanted" list of fugitive Nazis. Hank had no intentions of revealing Carol's true identity.

"I've gotta drive Hank to the airport and then get to the office. Things are hopping over there. Am I ever gonna see you there again?"

"Me, no, I'm disabled now," Gino said with a grin.

"Mr. Domenico, I once again must thank you for all your efforts," Hank said, shaking his hand.

"I'd like to say it was a pleasure but . . ."

"I understand. *Auf wiedersehen.*"

As they turned to leave, Hank held up a hand and began to dig into his old leather briefcase. Max rolled his eyes. It seemed that every time Hank dug into that briefcase, he brought back trouble.

"Max, I almost forgot about my bill," he said, pulling out a large manila envelope.

"I think the reward certainly covers it."

"Take it. It's just a token."

Max opened the envelope and saw that it contained diamonds. There must have been about fifty large diamonds about the size of his pinky nail.

"Oh no, I couldn't take this. It'd be blood money."

"Blood that was spilled from you and your partner. Your family was put through a lot. This will not make it all better, but maybe it will help. There is so much more than that. There are millions of dollars. Take it."

"I don't want to argue with you, Hank," Max said with a smile.

"Do you know the directions to the airport? I think we must cross the George Washingmachine Bridge."

As they walked down the corridor, Max put his arm over the smaller man's shoulder.

"Hank, you should have met my mother."

# Summary

I t is 1949.

Max Chambers, a not very successful private investigator based in his hometown of New Rochelle, New York, is forced to confront his wartime nightmare—the death of his childhood pal and the liberation of the infamous Nazi death camp, Buchenwald. With the help of his comical partner, Gino Domenico, and his plucky young secretary, Sally Connors, Max is faced with tracking down a war criminal, Karl Schmitt, the former commandant of Buchenwald.

Using clues provided by a former inmate of the death camp, Max and his crew face danger at every turn in an adventure that takes them on a whirlwind tour of the country. This is a case that threatens the happiness of Max's marriage and the security of his close-knit Italian family. Can Max bring this fugitive Nazi to justice? Knowing that execution is waiting for him, will Karl Schmitt kill again to avoid a visit with the gallows?

# Author's Biography

Michael was born and raised in New Rochelle, New York. He went to school and church and many of the other locales included in this book. He married his high school sweetheart and later moved to White Plains, New York. A life-threatening illness and subsequent complications ended a successful career in the banking industry and led him to a more creative outlook.

Michael is hard at work on a new Max Chambers adventure. He currently resides in Clarksville, Tennessee, with his wife, two children, and a pack of vicious dogs.

CPSIA information can be obtained
at www.ICGtesting.com
Printed in the USA
LVHW01s2125280518
578666LV00002BB/398/P